AF265539

The Slanderley Curse

Nuns and Mayhem in Cornwall

Clarice Stasz

Also by Clarice Stasz

Slanderley: Love and Murder in Cornwall

Jack London's Women

The Rockefeller Women: Dynasty of Piety, Privacy and Service

The Vanderbilt Women: Dynasty of Wealth, Glamour and Tragedy

American Dreamers: Charmian and Jack London

The Social Control of Deviance: A Critical Perspective (with Nanette Davis)

Female and Male: Socialization, Social Roles, and Social Structure

Sexism: Scientific Debates

Simulation Games for the Social Studies Teacher (with Samuel Livingston)

Simulation and Gaming in Social Science (with Michael Inbar)

The Slanderley Curse:

Nuns and Mayhem in Cornwall

Clarice Stasz

*"Appearance blinds,
whereas words reveal."*

Oscar Wilde

The Slanderley Curse

CONTENTS

The Slanderley Curse

To the Reader

Rarely do we find complete manuscripts composed by estate servants, let alone by Cornish servants. Herein, Kenal Gundry traces his southeast seaside origins to his service at Slanderley manor, perched on the rough northwestern coast. A pious lad, he shares his wonder at the lives of those to the manor born. Serving during the Edwardian Era, he comes of age during the rapid changes in society. His experiences in WWI are unconventional, thus add to our knowledge of that era.

Of special note is Kenal's appreciation of Slanderley's past. Though much family history was lost in the mist of time, he was intrigued by the story of the Nun's Curse, then watched its power snake through the manor during his tenure.

I should warn you of some grim episodes ahead, lightened by the droll and eccentric ways of Slanderley Manor. The oddities lie in the family lineage, as well as its Cornwall culture.

I must add this account needs what people in the United States would call Parental Guidance Advisement. Sections allude to bodily functions, albeit often in a subtle way.

In editing this manuscript, I have retained hints of Kenal's dialect. Despite being well-read, he was a terrible speller, so I corrected rather than *sic* him.

At times I was tempted to correct Kenal's factual errors, but I chose to keep them without comment. I also retain my British conventions in the U. S. edition, such as "Mrs" without a period, and could not avoid inclusion of favourite spellings common to our plucky island.

Dame Cecelia Scrivener
Winterfield College, Oxford University

A Fortunate Lad

When the wind whines like an ailing witch as it does tonight, I canna sleep. Like you, I have tricks and games to calm nagging memories. Betimes I count back slowly from a hundred and on good nights drop off before hitting eighty-three. I imagine myself lying in a skiff, the soothing laps of the waves calming me to sleep. Tonight, I choose to remember my childhood days by the coast in Cornwall. Come along with me, to ken my worries. I promise the story, early dark, will turn to better humor.

In case you have nae been here, peer at a map, and see that Cornwall is the big toe of Great Britain. The River Tamar separates us from Devonshire, and has long isolated us from the rest of the country. We donna consider ourselves English; we hold tight to our Cornish ways. Although the Romans came down, they little interfered, thus our ancestors kept fast to their ways and beliefs. We consider ourselves True Britons, for the great King Arthur were one of us.

The coastlines of Cornwall are most inviting, the southern section balmy at times, with palm trees and bright flowers to greet the visitor. Inland, the old mining region, can be rough and hilly. Full of granite and poor soil, dozens of rivers and streams rush down to kiss the sea in congenial bays. Our history prides its tales of fishery and smuggling skullduggery. You know: the Pirates of Penzance, charming onstage, kidnappers and enslavers at their actual.

I grew up in Mousehole [pronounced Muzzle] on the south coast, the fifth son of a fishing family, with two much older sisters. While they were short and wiry like rats, I grew brawny and big-boned with navy black hair, olive skin, and grey-blue eyes. My Tas [Dad] used to tease me that some Portuguese infected the family line a long time back. "The worm always do reappear," he'd chuff, "but on you tis handsome, Kenal Gundry."

With Tas being out on the boat, sometimes for many days, I little knew him. When he pushed in the back door, followed by my brothers, he'd hug me Mam before collapsing at the table to fill his very hungry stomach. After dinner, he'd go off for a time alone with her, or head out to the pub to meet his friends.

Things changed when I turned about seven. Because I grew big for my age, he early had me sort the catch. Like all those living in the small harbors, I reeked of salt, fish guts, and gull drops, but twere a perfume of honor. I longed to go out in the rough seas. Yet whenever I asked to go out, Tas said, "You be too young and would only get in the way."

As a result, I were very close to my Mam, who eased my tears when Tas denied me. I were always at her skirts while she stirred the chowder in the kitchen or picked gooseberries in the woods. She called me her "sweet lad" and I gloried in her light. She taught me how to repair nets, which led to patching my own shirts. She even showed me how to make the dough for pies.

She were a high-spirited woman, with sea-green eyes and shell pale skin. My first memory is of grasping her hand tight while we walked along Parade, the street fronting the waterfront. She was always talking, pointing out this or that on the ground, a plant or a wiggly bug. Born Annie Angwin, she grew up in Penzance, and had met my Tas while visiting Mousehole with friends. Her Tas was also a fisherman, so she knew the peculiar life ahead, one of days without him and worry over his return. Most of all, she were a devout Chapel [Methodist] woman, who saw to our good Christian upbringing.

When I were six, she sent me to school to learn letters and numbers. My name Kenal refers to *ken*, to know, and I proved to be a sharp student. Mam were pleased to see me succeed. My sisters, who used to read aloud to her, had long wed and left home, so I now sat by her at night to finger and say aloud words in the Bible verses. Mam knit in the candlelight, its flame glow deepening the wrinkles of her hardy face.

At school, I were cooped up with Mr Creakle and his heavy stick. While we lads struggled on our letters, he crept about the room soundless, as though afloat. His eyes were strangely glassy-colored, his thin lips an odd orange. His seldom smile revealed greenish teeth. He were a typical teacher, in other words, seen by us boys as ugly and shameful. While we feared him, he had one weakness. "S.s.s.students, take out your Arithmetic b.b.book." No surprise that away from class we mocked him. I did so once at home, saying "Mr C-c-creakle," and Mam smacked me face red.

Truth be, he ran a fair tutoring, one filled with interesting stories and adventures. He were patient while we struggled with inking our letters. In time, I understood his love of books, that there be a secret life within the bindings. Despite being a prankster, I did my reading and more. New words became a wonder, like conquering a twisty new knot. I were so good with my letters that I won a book of poems at the close of my first term. I may not write the Queen's English, but I can read it – just in case you don't believe me.

We be a close family. When weather was too blustery for the boats to go out, all of us, married children included, gathered at my sister Declan's large granite house on Parade. She'd wed the youngest son of the wealthy Victor family, the house a marriage gift. Her educated husband was the town clerk. Following an afternoon of chatter and games, my Tas would break into a chantey, my brothers and I soon joining in harmony. Our voices swelled almost-angelic while the women set to the evening meal and the youngest children napped. After feasting, Mam pulled me home because the men took to more singing with their brews. She did not approve of the drinking or the racy lyrics. Truth be, I were often tired and always needed some time to meself each day.

Now fishing is a dangerous livelihood, and was more so then, before fancy new instruments and knowledge of weather helped save lives. As babes, we all learned the story of town hero Tom Bawcock. Mam told it to me late one night while a fierce storm shook the house.

"Twere a terrible winter several hundred years ago, not long after the Spanish burned the town to the ground, along with all the boats. Years of sheer poverty followed, yet our townsfolk struggled and shared to recover. They'd rebuilt cottages, wove nets, and crafted new boats to fish and nourish all. Everyone worked together so no one family suffered worse than the other. At last a day came to be filled with hope for a full-stomach Christmas dinner, the first in ages.

"Alas, my lad, come November storms of fury lashed the town. Monstrous waves crashed over the sea walls, flooding the Parade, smashing masts and keels. The sun seemed stolen, never to return. No break broke the tempests. Families emptied their larders. Some stripped bark from trees to make into soup, for the deer and rabbits had fled into the highlands. Often people gathered daily in the Chapel to keep warm and pray for assistance.

"One day, during prayer, Tom Bawcock jumped up to shout, 'We are saved! The Lord has promised!' He pulled on his oilskin cape and dashed out into the howling downpour.

"What is happening, the people wondered. Tom were not the most able young man. Indeed, it were believed he'd bring poor luck to a boat. He never returned home that night.

"The next day at Chapel, during a silent prayer, including for Tom, a great shout pierced the walls. Tom's voice. 'Come, we are saved, come out!' Dashing into the yard, they saw him holding a basket of fish. 'There's much more at the boat. Go and share.' They were shocked to find a haul, seven kinds of fish, more than enough to feed the town for days. The women used them to make pies. A clever one stuck seven fish heads up from the crust, proof of the rich catch. That is what we now call Stargazy Pie."

Later I saw it as a story of hope, for I knew how the weather could turn ferocious, mighty Poseidon stirring up the seas. My Tas spoke direful tales of being tossed under an upturned boat, fearful he'd miss the surface in the black roiling water. This fret was rare for him, because he had the knack. He read the clouds and knew all the coves within safety. Unlike less careful men, he'd come in early with empty net or find a place to hide rather than dare the storm gods.

He were the same with boat rigging and net making, the sea crafts in his blood. They called him the best fisher in the tiny fleet. Other men sent their boys out with Hedrek Gundry to finish their training, for he could turn the clumsiest youth into a capable fisherman. No wonder I resented being kept away from all that skill and challenge.

When my years were about twelve, I were hanging some clothes in the yard with Mam, when what felt like a shower of frozen bullets hit our heads. The hail were so sharp it sliced the vegetable stalks and pierced the fruit. We heard glass breaking at the High Street shops down the slope. Lightening pounded like gunnery while we rushed indoors, our arms bleeding droplets from icy cuts. While we hugged under the kitchen table with furry Morvoren mewling in terror, we shuddered at the roaring rush of water overflowing the nearby creek.

After several hours passing, an early calm plumped down. The hail over, Mam and me ran to the bay, but we could not reach the shore. The Parade were flooded, the wharves torn apart from waves higher than we had ever known.

Our fear that something might happen to the fleet came true. Nearing dusk, a ragged half of the eight boats labored in, one by one, none being those of our Tas or me brothers. We hoped they'd found safety in Penzance. (Later we heard the storm in that town tore up the railroad tracks and even sank a large barge.) Under the dark night of the new moon, Mam and I returned home to light candles and pray for return of our two boats. Two days later we allowed they must have plunged to unmarked soggy graves.

That afternoon a neighbor came calling. She'd seen a boat limp in with two of my brothers aboard. They had left ahead of the small fleet on the day of the storm, and were far north of its main fury. Spying the clouds off to the south, they had pulled into a secluded cove. Relieved to see them, we celebrated through tears, being certain my Tas and two other brothers had gone down.

My poor Mam. Her widow watch had come true. She had little spirit left for other than grief. Too sad to do her chores, she slept or prayed the days away. By then I were as good at domestic chores as a girl preparing for marriage.

One evening Mam called me to her bedside with an odd request. "I want you to use the grace of God to guide us. Open your Bible without looking, put your finger on a line, and read."

I did so, and came to this passage:

60 Thou hast seen all their vengeance and all their imaginations against me.

61 Thou hast heard their reproach, O Lord, and all their imaginations against me;

62 the lips of those that rose up against me, and their device against me all the day.

63 Behold their sitting down, and their rising up; I am their music.

64 Render unto them a recompense, O Lord, according to the work of their hands.

65 Give them sorrow of heart, thy curse unto them.

66 Persecute and destroy them in anger from under the heavens of the Lord.

"Oh, Mam, it is from Lamentations. How can it help us with our grief? I'm not sure I understand."

Sighing deeply, after a long pause she said, "It is about people who are mean to us. Jeremiah is in the dungeon, and feeling helpless. He thinks God has deserted him."

"But he prays to God to punish the people who wrong him. That is not Christian."

She explained, "Nay, but it is very human to feel that way. Jeremiah comes to see that God will help those who are true to Him. So must we during our time of troubles, which are sure to continue. Promise me you will rise above that early anger and pray to Him for your own deliverance, not deliver pain upon those who hurt you."

I never liked Lamentations, and believed instead that this passage pointed to future difficulties. We'd enough of those, what with my Tas and two brothers dead. We didna even have their bodies to bury. Gruesome dreams of them rotting on the sea floor woke me up screaming. That we were not the only Mousehole family to lose loved ones in that wretched tempest brought us little comfort.

The usual time of mourning over, Mam called a family council. We gathered at me sister Declan's house, all our faces low and grey. My two remaining brothers, Conan and Goron, led the discussion.

"Before you tell us what to do, Mam, we have made up our minds. We will keep fishing. We repaired our boat so we can continue and take care of you. Even if we wed, we will see to your protection. We are firm agreed, and nothing you say will change our minds. We have seen the worst and know what it can do."

Before she could respond, I broke in. "Mam, I am old enough to go out with them. I can do more than fix nets and sort the fish."

"Ah, Kenal, I canna let you go. I long made a promise to your Tas that you never go to sea, no matter what happened."

I stood up and shouted, "What? Why would you make such oath? You know I love the waters. Did he think me not brave enough? Not strong enough?"

She said nothing while she poured some tea, the sign I should sit and listen.

"Nay, he respected you too much. He said one son must be free, which is why I insisted you do more school than the others. He saw a better future for you."

"But what can I do? I am not through school. I have not enough learning to set out. Who would hire me, a poor lad?"

"I will consult with the curate, and we will pray for an answer. God will guide us. I will also talk with Mr Creakle, who has more practical knowledge."

That were not a happy time for me. True, I were the best reader in the family, but I longed for a life with the burn of the brine. My brawny build would serve my skinny brothers well when pulling in the catch. I grew sulky and didna talk with my Mam during meals. My nightly prayers cursed Jeremiah and his weakly urge for forgiveness. What God had brought such tragedy to us? Must I bow to Him and ignore such disaster?

Several weeks later Mam returned from a visit with Mr Creakle to tell me my fate. Servitude was the only option for a whiskerless youngster like me. He had found me a place in service as the Hall Boy at Pennididdle estate, up near Bodmin Moor. Mam said she could move in with Declan's family, where she could watch the small grandchildren at play. Me two surviving brothers would keep the family cottage and continue to fish. I quickly consented. I need to free the family from caring for me.

Mr Creakle advised me on the life of service. He was lucky to escape it himself, for a childless uncle made him a ward and paid for full schooling. During breaks, he visited his parents at a manor house and recalled how they had little free time. He said service near sent his frail mother to an early grave until his teaching salary was able to free her from the kitchen. Their fate, he noted, was having employers lacking in Christian charity. While he knew nothing about Pennididdle, he wished me a better living.

The eve of my departing, our family gathered for a little farewell party. My brothers gave me a pair of new boots and a tiny travel Bible. My sisters packed work clothes they sewn for me into my old knapsack. Along with salt fish, Mam added my favorite pie, of mutton and apples, along with saffron cake.

The day I left was one of the worst of my life. For we all knew, we might never see one another again. Mam hugged me hard, then handed me her one good piece of jewelry, a pin my Tas had given her when courting. It were real silver, an image of loaves and fishes from the marriage at Cana.

"Remember you go in the comfort of the Lord. Obey your masters as you would him. That is your duty. And when your masters do ill, remember the consolation of Christ. So the Book says."

"Thank you, Mam," I choked. "I will send notes when I can. The Curate can read them to you and he can scribe your message back. God bless you as you bless me."

I threw the knapsack over my shoulder, turned away, and walked into town. I were too teary to look back.

The Slanderley Curse

A Dog Rescues

Mam arranged a horse cart delivering some goods inland to serve my passage. I sat on the hard wooden bench by the driver, and held on tightly to its edge while we bumped along. To ease me fears, I looked back down the sloping road to keep my eyes on the sea. In time, we were in dry woodlands, its grassy scents replacing that of salt and seaweed. I had been upland before to hear traveling Methodist preachers, yet being used to the wide expanse of the sea, the trees looming overhead uneased me.

The driver, the knob-nosed and bald Mr Penhale, were the chatty sort and sought to calm my twitchy legs.

"So you are off on an adventure? Tis not worth your frets. You aren't off to war nor the work house, as many a lad like you end up. You'll have food and a warm bed and new friends soon. Who can say you won't be by the sea again one day? Save your sorrows for your departed Tas and brothers, and think less of yourself."

"I know you mean well to comfort me, Mr Penhale, yet everything I face is new. I arrive with no ken of the work, the land, or the house. I am yet a boy."

"So you are, but that will change quickly enough. Do ye know nothing of your future?"

"Only that, except for the scullery maid, the house boy is at the bottom of the heap. I will lug coal, water, and more before the sun peeks up. I don't fear the hard work—"

"But you don't know about the people at Pennididdle. Let me fill you in.

"The grounds are vast and the house will seem grand, but be not deceived. The original English family came from up north. The Sextons were already rich through building the steam engines sold to our tin mine owners. One son took a liking to the area and decided to settle. A shower of coins blessed the family, so he bought some mines as well. He moved to Pennididdle and expanded the manor. It were once the center of local gentry's balls and grand dinners.

"Then came the fall. Do ye know why tin collapsed?"

"All I know is pilchards and nets. I canna imagine going under the ground to work. Isn't tin still in use? What happened?"

"Some explorers found big sources in Australia and other places. Even with shipping fees, tin is cheaper from there than from here. Ashamed by failures, the estate owner killed himself. Having only daughters, Pennididdle went to a distant American cousin and his wife, the Grubbs."

"The daughters got nothing? The family didn't share?"

"Not among the landowners. The firstborn son gets all. The estate goes to the next male relative, often a nephew. The Grubbs put on airs. They know nothing of our customs, nor of the management of the manor and lands."

"Are they cruel? Don't Americans own slaves? Am I to be *bound in chains*?" I recalled Mr Creakle's stories of slave owners beating their workers.

"Just be watchful when you arrive. Look to the other servants for advice and aid. I doubt you need fear chains."

"Mr Penhale, your story little calms me. You hint at a work house."

He laughed, then added, "Oh, no. I mean your employers are said to be fools. Idiots. They may more be amusement. Anyway, you will not often see them, if at all." He spit to punctuate his next remark. "They are, after all, Colonials, worse than Englishmen." I spit in agreement.

As the tired sun slipped toward supper time, Mr Penhale led the cart up a narrow drive boarded by wild shrubs and vines. It led to a hilltop stone cottage, its thatch roof in need of repair.

"Here's where I stay over on these trips and visit Nessa." Tossing a dirty quilt at me, he added, "You'll have to sleep on the ground. There's only one bed and Nessa does not take to boys, if you get what I mean."

I didn't.

The cart turned into a narrow lane bordered by a thick hedge that blocked my view. The way were very steep and scary. I breathed again when we stopped in a clearing at the top to reveal an old stone cottage. Its door opened to reveal a stout woman raising a jug while shouting, "It's time you showed up, you baldy old dog. You look as dry as a nun's fanny. Who's the dwarf? Bring him in too."

Before Mr Penhale could respond, I told him I would see to the horse and had me own food. If I wanted to get to Pennididdle, then I better not spoil his plans.

Later, strange cries came from the house, reminding me of the cat fights on the docks. To ignore them, I took out my Bible and read by candle light. I returned to the Psalms with their reminder to "Trust the Lord." I needed to trust Him to overcome my fears of the future.

Next day, Mr Penhale awoke me with a morning cheer. I crawled out of the cart, where I'd slept, and stretched my creaking bones. He handed me a pasty and a cup full of berries.

"Thank ye, sir. I hardly expected any treat."

"Nessa says you must be a good lad. I agreed, so we set on this thanks for the night's break. I trust you were comfortable enough."

"Oh, yes, the weather were sweet, and the cart long for my body. How many more days to Pennididdle?"

"The lane is dried out from the storms, so we should make good time and arrive this afternoon."

Pleased by that news, I helped Mr Penhale feed the horse and fit it to the cart. He proved right, for the road straightened as it followed the spine of the country. At times we could see the seas to the west and the channel to our right. Though I'd studied maps at school, I little understood how narrow our Cornish land be.

The ocean breezes sent up its special salty perfume. The day were so pleasant that I nodded off at times. So it be a surprise when I jerked awake, the cart having stopped.

"Here's where you go off, lad. Twas a pleasure with your company." I handed him his coins for passage, with an extra tossed in.

"Just follow that narrow lane through the woodland and you'll soon be at Pennididdle manor."

I wandered through the woody path, then into swards of grass with deer. I was in no hurry, for I had no experience with manor life. The narrow walk wove about until I turned past a large hedge of blood-red rhododendrons opening up to reveal the house.

I had never seen a grand home before, and could not grasp its immensity. Its long brick front suggested a boarding school, not the spot for one family's pleasure. Its many-windowed design and low roof were what I later learned was Georgian, but inside its low ceilings and beams came from much earlier, back to Queen Bess – or so explained the housekeeper one day.

My first mistake upon arriving was to knock on the front door. Even though he expected me, black-cloaked Mr Chiggers, the butler, gangly and shell-pale, gaped his beetle eyes at me with a loud "Shoo, shoo, boy! Already you break the rules!" He waggled his sausage finger at me. Right off I were wrong.

He called for Squimm, who turned out to be a footman. He seemed several years older than me, with pimply face and whelk ears. Instead of greeting, he sneered down at me with his lower lip pulled out, eyes pinched and chin up. Without thinking, I bowed while I thanked him. He just grunted and ordered me to follow him around to the back of the house.

I barely kept up with his long legs as I shadowed him on the gravelly path. He suddenly stopped and turned, causing me to plow into his outstretched arm. Reaching around, he pulled my shirt tail out of me pants and grabbed my knap sack. Burrowing inside, he pulled out the small silver brooch my Mam had given me on departure. "Pay for the privilege," he quipped, as he tucked it into his pocket. Then he shoved me down a stairwell to the house cellars. I knew then this dodgy sot were not to be my friend.

Oh, what Mr Dickens could write about my life there! I slept on a cot set within a musty brooms closet. That is, I actually slept and spent my hours there, when not on a chore.

A hall boy's first chore was boot and shoe polishing. Mr Chiggers told me to gather them from the halls last thing at night and clean them first thing in the morning."

"Here's today's collection. Take them in this basket into the scullery to polish."

I followed him into the scullery, its stone floor puddled and muddy.

Mr Chiggers handed me a torn and stinking leather apron. "Now get going."

I pulled the boots out and set them in pairs, then pulled a short stool over.

"Not on the floor! Lay some paper down from that pile."

I did so and reset the pairs atop.

"So where do we keep the polish?"

"Do you know nawt? Apparently not. You have to make fresh polish."

"Sorry, I know nothing of that. I come from fishing folk. We never polished our shoes, apart from spit and a rag."

Mr Chiggers walked to call out into the kitchen.

"Cook. Can you believe this new hall boy doesn't know how to make polish? I bet he don't read either."

Cook came out with a large brown book and handed it to me. Her face, red from the heat, bore a scattering of flour, as did her hands.

"This'll have your polish receipts, along with other ones you may have to make up. All the supplies are in that large green cabinet. Watch for the bottles with skull and bones."

"Thank you, Cook. I can read and do measures. Thank you, Mr Chiggers. I welcome your help."

"Humph. I'll be back to check your work."

Not a good way to start my new post.

Skimming the ragged volume, I found the receipt. The ingredients were sweet oil, vinegar, treacle, and lamp black. Twere not long before my hands and apron were splattered and rank from the mixture. To my surprise, the medicine worked well, once I found a good thickness. I decided to find old gloves to protect myself from the nasty mixture the next time.

My other role was to serve the servants. Given the loss of income in recent years, the Grubbs had not improved upon the lack of newer heating and plumbing. Mornings, I filled coal shuttles for the maids. I emptied the servants' chamber pots. I set their meals and cleaned up dishes and cutlery, eating after them as well. Being at the beck and call of the butler and head footman, I soon learned the order of the service. Did I meet the needs of a maid before the head footman, the men would box my ear and call me Mooncalf or Pilchard Breath. Lamentations was right: the Lord had chosen for me affliction.

As for the family above, for over a year I rarely saw them, let alone their fancy rooms beyond the green door. Squimm brought down the boots from upstairs for me to polish. Very rarely was I sent outside, so my skin grew pale. I also stank, being at the bottom of the infrequent bathing list. For many months no one used my name, and I was just Boy.

I learned more of the Grubbs through the maids' tattle during suppers.

"There is just the two of them. They sent their only child, a boy, to boarding school."

"So they do not need us much," I guessed.

"Were that true. He thinks himself a Duke, lies about on his sofa half the day when not ringing the service bells. We are constantly running up and down stairs. As soon as you deliver one thing, he asks for another. Count yourself lucky to be out of his call."

Another added, "Then he is off to the tennis courts. They'd been weedy for years, but his first order was to clear and repair them. He fancies himself the sportsman, though I doubt he ever held a gun. I don't know what he would do at a hunt. He seldom takes a mount, and then, only the meekest one in the stable."

"So what I was told is true, that he doesn't understand our ways."

"Yes. He is a crude Yank, while she is little better. She tries to be all friendly with us maids. Imagine her asking questions about our interests and our families! When we are trying to arrange flowers in the background, she comes over to help. She don't know her station!"

Even Mr Chiggers spoke up. "She is always inviting other gentry over without understanding the order of things. Fancy teas, tennis parties, formal dinners. It is all so, so *American*. We struggle with a narrow budget for all this folderol as well. The Grubbs don't understand how land-rich has little to do with coin."

"We do so much mending now," added a maid.

"I wear myself out just keeping the visible areas up," added the sole gardener. "The woods are falling into ruin as well."

The house keeper explained further. "The house is a devil too. It remains frozen in the old Queen Victoria's mourning style. The Grubbs' kept all the heavy furniture, which hides under scarves, moth-eaten Spanish mantillas, and wormy tapestries. Coal dust settles in the crevices of wood carvings and plaster. The rooms are painted in Queen's favored shades of brown, the drapes closed to block out any sunlight. It is like working in a mausoleum."

Twas no wonder the house servants were pale as sheep, thin-boned as rats. In time I would learn almost everyone was on the search for a position elsewhere. It could be I had the easier position. Hearing of their troubles soothed my own.

Well after a year in service, I met the couple directly. Cook had me repackage some rat poison into a tin to take it over to Wolfbane, who worked in the carriage barn. Because I had a few free minutes, I took the long way around, past the summer house and the tennis court. I startled when a ball came flying over the hedge and landed before my feet. I picked it up to toss back. Kenning little of the game, I was examining the flannel-covered ball when a harsh tinny voice pierced my ears.

"Hey, there. You found my ball. How sweet of you." Walking toward me was a skinny wheat-haired woman in white slacks with a thin white shirt baring her arms. "Don't toss it. I'll come over."

Her dress left me speechless. A woman in pants! Worse, she held out her hand as though to shake mine.

"Hallo! I'm Thelma Grubb, though you probably know that. I've seen you help the maids beating rugs in the yard. You are?"

While taking the ball from me, she clasped her spidery fingers around both my hands.

I was speechless. I had never been so close to a woman such as this, so brazen, so wafting of artificial scent and facial powder. Her lips were painted a scarlet Jezebel. Then she shifted her left hand to tousle her fingers in my hair!

"Cat got your tongue? What nice curls you have. I envy you, 'cus I'm stuck with rollers all night. I'm sure the maids are all vying for your attention. Do you have a sweetie?"

Shaking my head to provoke her to stop, I murmured, "Kenal Gundry, ma'am. Hall Boy."

"Hm, you don't look like a boy to me." She poked the tennis ball on my nose.

I suddenly thought, is this teasing? The woman of the manor is playing with me in a private, nay, ungodly manner? I stepped back. "Sorry, ma'am, I am late for my duties."

Another hawking voice, much lower, brawled out.

"What's this? Thelma, what is going on? You are delaying the game." That must be her husband, I guessed. His greying head peered over the privets, his queer square face brick red and sweaty from the sport.

"And you, there. What are you doing in this area? Shoo, get back to the cellars! How dare you."

"My fault, Harry," tweeted Thelma. "This sweet young man helped me find the ball. Here, catch!"

She had a strong arm and succeeded in tossing directly to him.

Before leaving, she leant toward me and whispered, "Hope to see you again soon." Then winked!

God save me from Americans, I prayed. Mam would never want me near such women.

I would like to say that was our sole encounter, but it was not. From this time, she called me to assist her with some invented chore. Noting her call, Chiggers advised me it was not normal for one of my lowly status to go to private quarters. Several days later he advised I must obey her, so I guess she'd had a word with him.

The first time, Thelma was lounging in her sitting room with a book, upside down, in her hands. She asked me to move a side table that she claimed was too heavy for her. Made of bamboo, I easily lifted it with one hand. She kept me there while she disagreed with various placements, yet it ended up where it stood originally. During this process she moved alongside me, laying one hand on my back or arm while she pointed with the other.

Similar encounters followed. One time she wore a flimsy dressing gown and seemed to wear nothing underneath. She even tried to ply me with sherry until she accepted I truly was a teetotaler. Whenever possible, I kept her door wide open to expose her vile behavior.

In time this sort of interchange passed.

"Come here, sweet boy."

"Ahem, madam."

"What are you afraid of?"

"Um, nothing, madam."

"I said *(louder voice)* come closer!"

Me shuffling nearer.

"Now is this so bad?"

"MADAM!"

Sounds of table pushed over as I run out.

Of all the worries about joining service, this had never arisen. Such horror, this ongoing punishment by the *lady* of the house.

Squimm's beastliness continued. Whenever I sensed his lanky ginger-headed body nearby, I slid into the nearest room. (During one such escape, I caught Chiggers abed with the scullery maid, and ended up with extra piles of silver-polishing the rest of the day.) When least expected, Squimm confronted me with some new filth to clean, such as his piss pot filled with some tarry substance. He was disgusting in other ways. Once he caught me from behind, his fingers on my neck, his hips imitating the pasture bull during its most active season. Rather than fight back, I swallowed my anger and played meek. It was the good Christian way, me Mam would say. I was sure she never imagined the sinfulness of some in that manor.

I learned later that Squimm visited the mistress behind closed doors. I tried to ignore what he might be doing alone with her, and clung to Scripture when ill thoughts stepped into me mind.

The maids liked to tease me as well, but they did so in fun, as if I were a younger brother. By the second year they no longer laid nastier tasks on me and welcomed me beside them at the servant table. They were also God-fearing and kenned my love of the Bible's ways. We collected together on Sundays to attend Chapel, and sometimes took long walks in a group in the afternoon. They didn't like Squimm either and feared he would be named the next butler.

When I could, I wrote to Mam. Here is a typical note.

Dear Mam,

The weather here is very lovely. We do not get the worst of the storms. I am getting nutty brown from being outside so much.

A travelling preacher came to a nearby field last Sunday. He spoke about holding true to the Bible as a source for study and discussion. God gave us reason for a purpose, he reminded, and we can rejoice in that gift, so long as we use it wisely. He had a wonderful voice, and asked the men to come up and sing some favorite hymns. As we did so, the clouds broke and we felt blessed.

My work continues well, and those in service are all kindly, as are the family members.

I miss you and everyone so much and pray for you all nightly.

Your loving son,

Kenal

I knew Mr Creakle would read this to her, so I was very careful about proper English. He wrote down her responses in his clear hand, so I received one each fortnight. Here is one sent to me at Pennididdle.

Dearest Kenal,

I wish you were here to read to me in the evening. I am very comfortable here at Declan's, though some days the little ones wear me out. Her boy is like his dad, quiet and sober, while the girls are full of mischief and loud in song. Each spoils me in kisses and hugs.

Were it not for Mr Creakle, I would have no one to read to me, the adults being too busy or tired, and the children not old enough. He does so some afternoons after his teaching ends. I thank the Lord every night for such a salvation. Other widows suffer much worse situations.

Your brothers returned with their boat overflowing pilchards. They had to hire someone to help them unload and get them to the drying hall. Conan is courting Frannie Fritz, and we expect a wedding before the year is out. Goron is looking forward to being a lone bachelor in the old cottage. At least we have kept our little home and plot to pass on.

This house is warmer and eases my aching bones. I can see the sea from my bedroom window, and still watch the boats go out and return. We've had no storms of late to make sad women and children.

I wish I could see you in such health. Friends are not a substitute for family, yet a solace, I am sure. Do keep telling me about the sermons you hear. Of all, I rejoice that you are so pious.

Yr. loving Mam

In time Cook warmed up to me. "You set a fine servant table for us," she said one day. "And you don't shirk the swabbing and drying of our dinner ware."

"Me Mam and Tas taught me to work hard," I replied, "and not be ashamed of the crudest task. Tis what the Good Book teaches."

"I could tell you had a holy upbringing. Alas, that's not the case for all in service. The lucky ones, like Mr Chiggers and meself, were born into the work. We had happy childhoods until we reached the age. Still, we take pride in what we learned and give thanks we are not in a poor house. Others, like Squimm, suffered terrible times, a drinking Tas and Mam who beat him. He seldom sat at a full table."

"That gives him no excuse to beat me," I argued.

"Nay, but mebbe make a prayer for him anyways. I can see you are a dutiful Christian."

Well, not enough to forgive Squimm, nor pray for him, I thought.

Just as Mr Dickens would not leave me in a dark fate, so must I be set free. It were a hunt weekend, if you can imagine Harry Grubb heading such. Some guests brought their house dogs for company. While the party was crashing out over fields, a German Pudelpointer broke out of the house, a terrible escape that could bring severe punishment upon us servants. It dashed down the south field toward the thickest woodlot, where it would be hard to find. I happened to be outside beating some dusty dresser shawls when I noticed the fleeing animal and took off after it.

As I rushed down the slope toward the milky pond, I felt as though flying, so free to be speeding in the sunny field. The dog suddenly stopped and dove into the water to head after some ducks. I had no choice but to follow, fully clothed, though I worried about the beast drowning me in its fury. Yet on my whistle, it simply stopped, turned, and swam over. It followed me out and joined me on the hike back to the house. We appeared in full dripping state up the entrance drive as the hunt group rode in.

Chiggers was at the open doorway, swooshing his arm at me to run fast away, out of sight. I fled the wrong way, toward the back veranda and gardens, then ducked behind a statue. I had never viewed a hunt group in full colors before. I almost giggled at the sight of Mr Harry in garish scarlet coat on a shrimpish mare. Unlike the others, who were fully asweat, he seemed freshly dressed. I doubted he had done little, just head out at the start, hide in a copse, and rejoined the hunt's return.

Meanwhile, the Pudelpointer, staying behind, shook his dripping fur all over a close by mount, the man atop laughing. "Gwandror, how did you get out, you naughty boy?"

He dismounted and shushed the dog indoors. So atremble that I nearly wet my pants, instead I exploded a loud thunderous sneeze. Then, bad luck, a second.

"Who is there?" cried a whiney-voiced hunter. "Come out and show yourself."

Exposed, I had no choice but to creep out from behind, my head bowed upon my chest.

"You! I should have guessed," barked Mr Grubb. Turning his head back toward the others, he added, "It's the lazy do-nothing I told you about."

Mr Chiggers roared. "Boy! What are you doing outside? I'll see he's mightily punished, Sir."

I be too scared even to peek up at those speaking.

"Punished? Pack him off at once!" Mr Grubb growled.

I stood tense and blind until the sound of the riders left the scene. Then I rushed about to the back, down the cellar, and gathered my few belongings into my knap sack.

Where could I go? I would be lost here, hopeless to tell directions. The route up was so twisted and branched that I'd little hope of retracing my way home. I resisted that path, ashamed of what my family would say.

Squimm came by and laughed. "Tossed out? No surprise. It's getting late, so watch out for the Knockers. They creep out of the old mines at night. They'll stomp you down and call a raven to eat your eyes while you are still alive."

"The same to you," I replied, shocked by my unexpected comeback. Standing up, I realized I had grown and stood over him now. Why'd I let him come at me so? It be a relief to get away, even with the frightening Knockers and Piskies haunting the Cornish woods.

He laughed back, "Ah, but I still have yer fancy pin. You'll never see that again!"

Just then Cook appeared. "Get off, Squimm, and check the table setting upstairs. You're late already."

Turning to me, she shook her sheep-wool head. "He's to get his Devil's curse one of these days. Go to the scullery. I've set some food to get you off with a full belly, and some roots to see you for a couple of days on the road."

Before I could thank her, she spun around, her sauce-streaked skirt swaying as she returned to the kitchen.

In the scullery, I found a bowl of white soup of an oniony taste, a plate of fish, a joint of mutton, potatoes with strange jellies, some raw greens, and a pudding. This was for the upstairs dinner! I had never eaten so well in my life! As promised, a cloth bag held roots and hard fruit, ready to ripen while I hiked.

While I was in the Butler's Pantry cleaning my dishes and cutlery, Mr Chiggers appeared.

"Ahem, I am asked to bring you to the terrace. Someone upstairs requests your appearance." His pursed lips and red face gave away his feelings.

"Who?"

"Just follow me," he growled.

We went not up the service stairs into the house, but outside and around the grounds to the terrace. A gentleman sat alone there with the Pudelpointer resting beside him. Mr Chiggers shoved me forward and left. I bowed while averting me eyes.

"Come closer, Boy, so I can speak quietly. I mean no harm."

I moved in and glanced at his face, long, tanned, and of small chin. Though he clenched a stern mouth, his dark eyes sparkled in the sun under lobster-colored locks.

"Sir," I bowed again.

"I understand you are the one who brought Gwandror out of the lake. He is young and headstrong and needs close watching. The point is I know you are not to blame for his escape."

"Thank you, sir." I watched for his sign that I leave, yet none came.

"I know you have been let go. I could argue for your staying here, but I have an offer. My own House Boy is leaving. I should like you to join my household. Your name?"

I didna know what to say. I had not found service pleasant. I didna want to continue sleeping on the floor and eating the dregs of the service meals. Yet dare I try to return home, where I would be more trouble than help? I'd return in shame and add another stomach for my family to feed.

"Yes or no, Boy?"

"Oh, thank you, sir, I am speechless from your offer. Yes, please, I welcome your position. My name is Kenal Gundry."

He petted Gwandror while adding, "I leave tomorrow and will send a cart to bring you later. There is an inn up the main road. Go now and leave before anyone hears of your new position. Take this for travel."

Grasping the shiny coin, I squeezed back tears. I did not know my new family's name, nor the place, yet I sensed a good prospect.

The Slanderley Curse

Sea at Last

Given my instructions, I slunk off without further farewells. Within several hours I reached the Dead Tinman Inn, a white-washed and thatch-roofed dwelling edging the lane. When I entered the warm open-hearth room, the burly host seemed to be expecting me. Coming from behind the bar, he held out his hand for a shake, an honor I hardly expected. I was, after all, shabby and astink following my long hike.

"You must be Mr Gundry. I'm Mr Gummow. Go up the stairs to the first room on the right. I'll send up tea. You must be hungry after your travel."

"You're too kind, sir. I didna expect such a warm greeting. I am but a lowly boy in service."

"That may be so, but your employer has seen well to your care while you wait. I daresay you have *interesting* days ahead of you. Now go settle in and I'll explain more after dinner."

Entering my room, I faced a most inviting vision. Like the ground floor, it held a beamed ceiling and a small hearth already afire. The bed were large enough for a well-fed couple, covered with an embroidered spread. A desk holding an ink pot and a sheet of paper overlooked the window. It tempted me to sit down and make notes of my travel, which I did. So started this story.

The tea arrived, along with fairings [ginger biscuits]. I soon fell drowsy and awoke to darkness, hoping I had not missed the evening meal. Downstairs, I sat alone to enjoy the mutton stew in privacy, Mr Gummow soon joining me after setting down two large mugs of ale. His wiggling cheeks were painted red from the heat of the room.

"When you're done with that, there's more. Here, drink hearty!"

"Thank you, sir, you do me so many favors, but I am not one for the ale."

"Oh, you be a serious Methodist then? You are missing out on some fine pleasure, my lad." He followed this with a full empty of his flask, punctuated by a large cow-like belch. "I'll not force you, for I now have the second to meself. Meanwhile, may I speak of your future? Do you have any questions?

Finishing my bowl, I admitted full ignorance. "I only met milord for a quick talk, though his character seemed kindly. His delivering me here points to his generous nature. I am but to be in his service, yet he treated me well."

"That is so, you ken correct, though you may not find all others of the family so formed. His wife is, I dare say, *muskok,* [crazy], but harmless. You need not fear her. The others are sane though be not quick with wit."

"How is that?"

"Those manor folks mix up their lines so much," he asserted. "At house parties, do you know, they skulk about their bedrooms at night and switch partners? All that sneaking about the hallways! Who knows who fathers the children!"

"But they can't all be like that. Not all," I challenged. "So where does the slow brain come from?"

"Well, not from the original family a century ago. They was sharp about getting and keeping rich. While bad times in the mines crushed others, they added to the manor and lands. Their solution was to bring over rich and silly American wives," he explained. "After all, who settled that corrupt land across the seas except crooks and fifth sons? Colonials, bah! We were good to lose them."

"Could be," I agreed. "For who would a family send over, never to be seen again, but the dunce or idiot in the line?"

"T'were clear from the start that these wives missed a key cog or two. Born here, they'd have ended up in Bedlam."

"So what does the current Lady do that is so odd?

Before he could answer, the door burst open with a handful of high-spirited visitors. Mr Gummow's account left me more confused than prepared.

Two days later, most of it spent in rest, a fancy carriage appeared to take me to my new position. The coachman, scrawny as an eel in an oversized maroon jacket, introduced himself as Gleeves.

"You must be the new boy. Climb up here besides. We've a long ride, but the roads are good and the weather dry. What's your name?"

"Kenal Gundry, sir. Excuse me, I don't know where we are heading."

"Don't call me 'sir.' I'm in service like you. I'm head coachman, not that there are other coaches, so I must be head by necessity. We will first stop at the town of Slyme Gurney before reaching the nearby estate of Slanderley. It's up on the north coast by the Celtic Sea, a wild area attracting only the hardiest folk."

You can imagine my delight upon hearing I was returning to water. I imagined salt and fish, furious storm-tossed tides, and deaths by drowning. I could not help but laugh in glee.

"Slyme Gurney cozies in a half bowl on the hillsides inland from the Bay of Piskies," he added. "It has a couple of shops, pubs, and a church. Twere larger many years ago."

"Methodist?" I inquired.

"Nay, there is a Chapel shared by nonconformists and most of the townsfolk, and an Anglican church for local gentry and visitors to the estate. Not that many arrive, for the trip is difficult for Londoners. They take the fast train to Plymouth, then a noisy local to Bodmin, followed by an uncomfortable carriage ride. It is the duty I most dread, for when a big hunt weekend is planned the repeat trips shake my bones like a bass drummer, even though this one is a good carriage."

"I do ken. I had to travel from Mousehole to Pennididdle solely by cart. Though this be a worse road, it be nae so harsh."

"Aye, it's the springs. Be it raining, I'd have set you inside though it is not so nice there. One man smoking and it be miserable to the other travelers."

Hours later, we arrived at Slyme Gurney. As Gleeves said, it were barely a village, a few houses and the stores facing right up to the road. He pulled over by the butcher shop to collect a package.

"We raise our food, but Cook wanted chicken livers for the cats, and we didn't want to slaughter our own hens to spoil the mewing ratters. If nothing else good comes to you, count on hearty meals. Not that you should expect anything bad, I mean."

His remark had the dark hinting sound of Mr Gummow referring to the place as "interesting." I needed to follow up.

"Yet the estate is called Slanderley. How did that name come about? It sounds odd, even mysterious."

"Ah, don't let your worries take over. Tis a lovely house and land. We in service take care of one another, I can assure you. We don't snipe and argue as at other manors. Anyway, we are almost there."

We had mounted to a height from where I could see the sea in the distance. On a cliff above a small cove hovered a large U-shaped manor with a scatter of sheds and barns behind the open U. Further beyond were fields and a large woodland.

"Everything you see in all directions below is the estate, all the tenanted fields included," noted Gleeves with a sweep of his arm. "We arrive just in time for tea. You'll soon ken why your worries are but a nit."

After the carriage swirled down the ridgeline, we came upon a small stone house next to a large iron gate. "That's for the rare times we have to check visitors in, during a large event, for example. For now it houses the Quirk sisters, and one's son, Eddie. Jemima Quirk is the estate secretary and overall assistant to his lordship. She is sharp, yet kindly. Her sister is house keeper. She too is kindly but will watch your work carefully."

We crossed through the open gates onto a well-graveled road that passed through a large wooded area. Upon leaving the trees, the view opened up to reveal a large lake on the left, a sprawling lawn on the right. Some sheep waddled in the grass toward the tree edges.

"When you go out on the lawn, watch for the ha-ha. For much of it you can leap over, but some parts are very deep with rock at the bottom."

"Ha-ha? Are you teasing me?"

"Nae. It's a ditch to keep the animals below the lawn adjoining the manor. A kind of upside-down fence one can't' see. So it really should be 'ah-ah.'"

We soon entered a large area with a circular planting and fountain of spouting dolphins in the middle. At the far end stood the house, its face long and majestic, with matching rows of windows gleaming in the sun. Gleeves directed the carriage to the left, on a narrow path between a side wing of the house and a cliff edge overlooking a cove below. I became dizzy peering out, then breathed the chilly sea air in deeply and shut my eyes in pleasure.

At the back end of the manor, Gleeves identified the array of sheds and buildings I'd noted from above.

"There's the laundry, the stables, the forge, and cottages for the outdoors men. When an earlier owner added the wings, he forgot they would enclose the kitchen garden and chicken yard. Most fancy houses would have more gardens and fountains there, but we be nae fancy. The chickens moved, but as you see the vegetables remained, apart from the flowery spot and statues by the back patio."

"I'm sure the cook likes having the food so close by."

"I'll drop ye at the back entrance. Someone will meet you at the bottom of the stairs to the service floor. He will settle you in."

"Thank you, Mr Gleeves. I do keep you in my prayers."

"Thank ye, but I've no need of ghostly help."

In the service floor hallway stood a young tow-haired man dressed in rough clothes, so I knew he wasn't a footman. He extended a long-fingered hand, his hard grip hinting at his strength.

"You must be the new house boy. Call me Snerd. I be the general all-abouts for the gardener and coachman. I'm to show you about."

"Thank you. Yes, I'm Kenal Gundry, just up from Pennididdle. How kind of you."

"No troubles. Leave your sack here. Right now most all is down on the beach. The family are holding a small tea party for local friends down there. Follow me so I can point out who's who. Later I'll introduce you to the chap sharing your room in the attic."

A real bed! Gleeves was right.

Snerd explained we would take a backway down the cliff side and linger where we couldn't be seen. When I mentioned I hadn't eaten since early morning, he took me into the walled kitchen garden, where he pulled up some gritty young carrots for a snack. After we washed them off at the spigot, I bent down for a long drink. As Snerd turned on the faucet, I noted he had lost the tip of a pointer finger, perhaps during his work.

He led me to the top of what seemed a dangerous precipice, a sheer rock drop to the scramble below. Down the beach to the left was a long cottage, a boat shed, and a collection of well-dressed people gathered by the two structures. I could hear their chattering though not the actual words.

Being used to flatland, I was a bit dizzy and took my first step down slipping with fright. Snerd was not only agile, he showed me how to locate safe hand grips, to move only when I had three points under control. I was soon sweaty from nerves, my palms scoured raw. Upon reaching bottom, he led me to the back of the cottage, where, peeking from a corner, I watched the party underway close up. I had never seen anything like it before. Nothing was ever set like it at the Grubbs' tennis parties.

Several thick and colorful carpets provided protection from the rocky sand underneath to shape a kind of room. Upon it perched a long linen-clothed table. A large silvery tea urn sat at one end, a variety of layered plates with fluffy iced finger cakes and tiny sandwiches alongside. A maid in black dress and white apron floated about with a tray to serve and to collect cups for refill. The cups were so thin that one could almost see through them.

A purple-coated footman stood by the urn to assist a flax-haired woman dressed in a pink gown with a lacy jacket. Stuffed birds perched upon her enormous hat. Her lips pinched while she carefully poured, her yellow cat eyes asquint. Her long face was unseemly pale, and her chin was what I recalled from science class as *prognathous*, the kind of big word that describes what it means.

"The one serving is Lady Gladys," whispered Snerd. "She came from New York to wed Lord Leo de Loverly. Without her dowry that solid silver urn would have been sold and replaced with cheap plated silver. Her arrival has made life much better for everyone on the estate, tenants included. The Chipchap manor owners at nearby Bude had to sell their entire library to someone in the Colonies, while Pennididdle is slowly falling apart, as you well know."

"She seems a bit uncomfortable, her hands ashakey. Isn't this *her* party, she be hostess?"

"Aye. She's a good woman, though often off by herself. That is, apart from meetings with some special lady friends. There's his Lord, the ginger-hair, with the men over by the boat house."

I recognized His Lordship from our brief meeting in Pennididdle. He was shorter than his wife, and contrasted more with his sturdy body and tiny chin. He was laughing full blast at some apparent joke. I wondered at the men's fancy suits and top hats, the funny white covers on their shoes. Another man walked over, dressed in what I later learned was a golfing suit, strangely short pants and long socks. Hands shook about, and more laughter followed.

I pointed to two children, a toddler in a sailor suit and a girl perhaps four or five, in a long cotton dress with pinafore. "Algernon and Letitia," explained Snerd. "The heir, but no spare, no backup son, yet. Privately we say Algie and Letty."

Algernon shared his father's red hair and chinless face, while Letitia copied her mother's narrow, pale look and large chin, though with green eyes. The boy held a small racket, and was using it to hit stones toward his sister. Then a short woman in grey service dress grabbed the racket in one hand, his arm in the other, and pulled him toward the cottage. She opened the door and pushed him inside.

"Ye'll stay in there until I say so. Ye wicked, wicked boy! Go in and sit on the chair next to Mrs McCrae."

"That's his nanny, Mrs Cameron. Do ye know that means Crooked Nose? Fits her, nae? The lad needs a firm hand. Letty is a sweet one, though. She is fond of horses, so you will find her around the stable yards. Tis fine to chat with her if she comes by. And there's Mr Bunston, the butler, who you'll meet in the dining hall later."

My new boss was tall, seemingly boneless, with straggly hair and sea blue eyes. He stood quietly in the background, his face a mask, his eyes flickering here and there to see all was running smoothly. I hoped he were not like Chiggers, too strict and fussy.

"He'll not bother you much," Snerd noted, as if reading my thoughts. "He is said to be the bastard of a distant de Loverly cousin. The Quirk sisters really run the place."

"Yes, Mr Gleeves told me about them. Tis a strange arrangement."

In time, Lady Gladys left the urn to the footman and floated toward a cluster of women sitting in their tiny chairs like a pool of fish, their gowns glistening like scales in the sun. They seemed to be discussing their strange hats, for they were pointing to this or that ornament. One wore something different, a straw bowler trimmed with a tartan ribbon, and took it off so others could examine it. The conversation stopped when a monstrously large woman dressed in a deep purple gown approached them. Faces tightened.

Mr Snerd explained. "The Bishop's wife, imagines herself all better than everyone. A tattle as well. Bungs her way into every social, asked or not. Was asked here, by Lord Leo, not her Lady. The Bishop is his good friend. Lady Gladys is none-too-fond of either."

"So the Lord is a true friend of Christ? I am pleased to know that."

"Well, I can't say that is so. He and the Bishop do enjoy their cigars and sherry together. His wife always carries a bag filled with candies and cakes, which she eats without a share and smacks her lips. As you might guess, she has a tin miner's appetite. The Bishop is one of those younger sons fobbed off onto the church life. I can't say any about his faith as I am a Chapel man meself."

"So shall we have prayers nightly in the servant hall? Pennididdle did not, though I heard other houses run on such practice."

"Apart from a dinner grace, nae. Speaking of which, the sun's fall to sea signs we must head back. Follow me to the water. We'll get our feet wet, but if we walk near the party, they will pretend not to see us. I'll lead you up the real beach pathway."

We rolled up our pant legs, removed our shoes, and waded out in a wide circle past the gathering. As Mr Snerd described, they didna see us, but they did.

By day's end I were exhausted. Mr Snerd introduced me to Mugwatch, the footman whose room I shared. He were much older, with dirty straw blond hair and the empty grey eyes of a dead cod. The opposite of Squimm, he seemed unbothered to share and kindly showed me about.

Our room was on the ground floor. "To keep far away from the maids upstairs," explained Mr Snerd.

Mugwatch took over at that point. "Here's the storage chest you can use. You'll find extra bedding down the hall. The cots are fair good, so you will sleep well.

"Thank you. What are your main duties?"

"I serve the couple's meals and assist Mr Bunston as needed. You will serve upstairs table only when there are visitors, which is not often."

"I have not served before, only been a House Boy."

"Mr Bunston and I will train you. Speaking of which, you need to gather your work uniforms.

He led me to the clothing storage room where I found two sets of trousers, some shirts, and a hat. They were not fancy, yet of good material and in the estate's colors of maroon with pink touches.

"Though we are not a grand estate, Lord Leo likes us to keep up top appearances. I suggest you do a better trim of your whiskers and keep your hair neater. You are no longer a House Boy hiding below stairs."

"This is so different from Pennididdle, where the maids had patches on their aprons."

"Augh, that excuse for a fancy manor. At least the Americans who came to Slanderley were of high class."

"Excuse me, I am not sure what to call you. I was called Kenal at Pennididdle. If I use your first name, what is it?"

"Just use Mugwatch. That's enough."

I was grateful to have so helpful a work companion. Later I would learn this was the longest conversation we would ever have.

My first servants' dinner introduced me to both outside and house workers, and ran with ease by Mrs Quirk, the house keeper. She were a middling sort, with middling brown hair, and a middling face. After leading Grace, she introduced me and had the others do the same. Next to Snerd (I was told to drop the Mr) sat Turgid, another outdoors worker. He offered a lopsided grin as he peered at me through his bulging and wandering eyes. Alice of the long flaxen hair was the top maid, with Jane as her assistant. ("Not my actual name," she said, "but it is what they called me at my last place, and it seemed to stick.") Mugwatch sat beside them, pressing into Jane's shoulder. Gleeves raised a bone in recognition, while Mr Bunston slumped in his chair at the head of the table.

The food was much heartier than at Pennididdle, this night both fish and mutton, with a berry pie. How could this be? When younger, I had heard fearsome tales of service life.

Snerd was to show me around more outside the next morning, while Mrs Quirk would go over the house schedule in the afternoon. It seemed she had more power than the butler, who strangely silent at dinner. Mr Bunston's formal introduction extended a flabby paw and grunt of greeting. I learned later that he was more like the Lord's valet and personal aide and seldom played butler apart from announcing guests.

Once in my room, I knelt to pray before sleep. After greeting me, Mugwatch said nothing more. Once in his night shirt, he snuffed his candle and turned over to sleep, soon puffing like a child's steam toy. The cot were most comfortable with its heavy coverlet. I meant to read some Bible, but asked for forgiveness and went fast to sleep meself.

More Mysteries Emerge

Up at dawn, with no boots to clean, I went down to the kitchen, where Mrs Viscous, the cook, showed me about so I could do service dishes after breakfast. She were young and jolly. Despite having all the many meals and baking to prepare, she had only a "daily" in from the village to help her out by kneading and slicing, as needed. The house scullery maid were brawny from all the lifting and cleaning of heavy pots. Mrs Viscous were proud of her kitchen and its orderliness, a place for each iron pan or copper pot.

Handling the servants' breakfast dishes cheered me. The warm suds reminded me of days with me Mam, helping her when my Tas and brothers were off at sea. I could hear Mrs Viscous singing in the kitchen and began to hum along. She'd a sweet voice and sang ditties I'd learned in school, tunes full of fun and sunshine.

Snerd arrived as expected and told me to prepare for a good morning's hike. First he took me to the boot room to find me a spare pair for the trek through the damp grounds. Then he marched me around the east wing with its large patio overlooking the immense spread of lawn dotted with fat wooly sheep at the distant border. He led me out down the lawn to point out the edges of the ha-ha.

"As you can see, most of it is easy to cross, a long stride or a short leap." Then he pointed me where the ha-ha met the entrance drive. "Here it is much deeper with a rocky bottom to drain rain water under the road through a pipe into the lake."

We crossed the road over to a footpath by the lake. A few ducks showed off their rears as they dabbled for breakfast, while some gulls flew overhead, cowling like anxious ghosts. Two gulls dove over our heads and splatted us in greeting. The pathway led into the woods, taking us face up to a stone pyramid about seven feet high.

"An old hermit's hut," snorted Snerd. "The previous Lord were fond of housing solitary men, though he really wanted them for entertainment, if you get what I mean."

"Oh, to play Chess and such games?"

"Ah, not quite. A different sort of encounter. You get what I mean?"

Puzzled, I dropped further questions until we came upon a large mill cottage alongside a creek flowing into the lake.

"Did you grow wheat here? I see the wheel no longer turns."

"Nae, this is another folly, a kind of house for special guests. Never go inside though. It is haunted by those who died there. Horrible corpses, they was. I wouldn't know. I only heard the stories. Ripped to pieces," he sniggered with a hint of glee.

I hesitate to describe the next foolish folly: a gigantic hedgehog sculpture with a door leading into its backside.

"Another hermitage?" I suggested.

"Aye, also used by some special guests. But we now keep it well-locked. I am in charge of keeping all the follies closed up for safety. Only I hold all the keys."

"Because it is haunted too?"

"No, because it is cursed."

Curiouser and curiouser. We Cornish love our folk tales with their fairies, piskies, and spirits. We pass dark winter nights spinning tales of their frightening forces. When so many men lose lives too young to mine collapse or dark salty depths, we keep death close to heart. I decided Snerd was playing with me in a similar way and did not question.

In time, we encircled the entire lake to meet a miniature Greek temple not far from the manor. Inside were comfortable lounges and tables facing out toward the pleasing sight of sparkling water and fluffy swans drifting so peacefully.

"The summer house," he explained, "for warm evening conversations."

"And I should not enter."

"Nae, it is perfectly fine. Not you, because you are a servant, unless someone orders you there. Behind the porch is another room. A good place for young lovers, if you get what I mean."

I didn't get his point. I was distracted by what seemed to be the swift movement of a nun's robe flit in the darkest part of the structure, but Snerd pulled me off before I could comment. We passed the house on the cliff path, where I noticed a large stone bench.

"If you want a quiet moment, this seat is permitted as it is out of sight. Stay away from the other side of the path on top of the cliff. What looks like firm ground may have nothing underneath."

"If it is dangerous, why is there no fence?"

"Have we not brains? We're Cornish!"

The rest of our tramp took us to the many work buildings beyond the service entrance: the barns, carpenter shed, blacksmith lean-to, laundry, drying house, buttery, and more. In addition to Snerd and Gleeves, few other men worked outside. We chatted with Turgid, who explained that he managed the woods, trimming brush, picking mushrooms, and setting traps. Snerd handled small outdoor repairs as well as minor gardening and shepherding of the sheep.

"Excuse me. Pennididdle had a larger staff yet was smaller. How does Slanderley manage?"

"We hire the local workers from Slyme Gurney when needed. We have few social events, and call in others from the village to fill in for those. Most of the manor food comes from the kitchen garden and from tenants," explained Turgid. "The land is good and the tenants do not slack."

I doubted that, yet held silent. How could lands so buffeted by the ocean storms produce much? Then again, I were a fisher folk, not a farmer's boy. Later I learned of hedges and copses protecting fields of grain, small herds of sheep and cattle, vegetable plots, and berry vines.

Snerd led me to the most disheveled shed, where we found a man called Sloth, who be busy sharpening the teeth on an animal trap. He were easily mistaken for a Traveler, being dressed in layers of ragged clothes with a scarf tied at his neck. I noticed his front teeth were also sharpened to points.

We didn't converse. As Snerd explained, "The poor man slid over the cliff one night. He survived, but was out for many days. He is sometimes himself, sometimes not. But he be harmless and wise about the animals in the woods."

"His teeth?"

"Ah, yes. After the accident he filed them down. He said he were half fox. He's no fan of the hunt, though we keep that secret from Lord Leo."

Following lunch, the housekeeper ordered me to join her. Having reached my adult height, I towered over her. Keys jingled off her belt, her only jewelry a watch pinned upside down on her immense bosom so she could check the time quickly.

"We may seem more lax than your last position. Flexible, of necessity. Being so isolated, we require a particular type to work here. For example, this is a family of riders, so keeping up boots is a major task. You may be called for any variety of chores as our needs develop. Do see you get a valet suit from the storeroom. We seldom have formal dinners with guests, but you must step in when we do."

"I like what you say very much, "I replied. "I had different chores at home that changed with the season. I come from a fishing family, so I am at ease with hard work."

"I am pleased to learn such. Otherwise, I would have sent you right away. Lord Leo may have hired you, but I can fire you with a snap of my fingers. Understand?"

"Yes, Mrs Quirk. But what of Mr Bunston? Wouldn't I normally be under his charge?"

"Let's just say he defers to me for other reasons. Now let's go up to the main house. If we see any of the family, be quiet and stand behind me. I understand Snerd pointed them out yesterday so you will recognize all four of them along with the Scottish nurses."

She led me up the service stairs through the green baize door into a large hallway. She explained the family apartments were in the first floor west wing overlooking the ocean. The east wing kept a few bedrooms shrouded for the rare guests, the reminder used for storage.

We started on the ground floor, where she rushed me quickly from one public room to another. There were drawing rooms of different sizes, and dining rooms, one formal, one for family, a library, a den, an estate business office, a morning room, a trophy room, and assorted closets. We entered few.

She did lead me to the main saloon. A wall of glass doors led to a large veranda overlooking the sweep of lawn. The room were so different from Pennididdle's dark and heavy décor. Light-colored silks graced the walls, while ceilings in the largest rooms shone with painted images of mythical creatures in nature. Some chairs had golden curvy legs and sat low to the ground.

"French," Mrs Quirk noted.

"They don't look very comfortable," I whispered.

"When Lord Leo's mother, Lady Peony Rockenastor arrived, her first order was to replace all the cumbersome dark furniture and heavy velvet drapes. She replaced it all with this Froggy style, Louie Cans, I think. It was very popular in New York mansions. Besides brightening the rooms, the gilded chairs are actually very comfortable."

I was tempted to try one but knew better.

She continued, "As part of the marriage contract, Lady Peony demanded the latest plumbing for their apartments and the kitchen. Then, upon her arrival, Lady Gladys convinced Lord Leo to convert the fireplaces and wall lighting to gas. She was trying to convince him to convert the water mill to bring in a bit of electricity as well, but so far she has been unsuccessful. So you see we are very modern in most regards, though I'd like wired lighting. Gas and candles become so troublesome "

She led me to the broad grand stairway, spreading her arms wide in praise. Above on the landing, a life sized portrait of a young black-haired women in a flouncy white dress peered down at us. She were so beautiful that I held my breath in wonder.

"An ancestor?" I asked.

"The Hussy," Mrs Quirk hissed. "Proof beauty can hide grievous sin."

Another mystery to uncover?

On the first floor, Mrs Quirk merely pointed to the doors to the private family apartments in the West Wing, which she advised I would seldom enter for they were the reserve of Mr Bunston and head maid Alice. A series of chinless gingers and horsey faced brunettes followed me as we walked the long portrait gallery linking the two side wings. Each room in the east wing was decorated according to the color scheme of its name: Horseradish, Gherkin,

Prune, and such. The furnishings seemed older, though very comfortable.

We took narrower stairs to the second floor west wing rooms, the quarters for the children and their minders. The nursery was immense with large open windows. The array of bookcases, work tables, and art easels hardly filled the space. Because each nurse and charge were at different ends of the room, we just peeped in. It was obvious the children were taught to put everything away, for no toys or books sat scattered on the ground.

"It is so orderly here," I remarked. "It seems as though no one uses it."

"Ah, those Scottish nurses. They are verrrrry strict. There are more lessons here than play. They insist windows be kept open even in the chill of winter. Algernon will head off to a boarding school in a couple of years, but Letitia will remain under dismal rule. The ladies are strict Calvinists," she said with a pruned nose. "They are always into the darkest books of the Bible, like Job."

Mrs Quirk could not know that I would welcome any friend to the Holy Book, so I kept quiet to stay in her favor.

Back down at the business office, she led me in to meet her sister, introduced as Jemima Quirk, and left me there. Short and of typical Cornish coloring, Jemima (so called herein to distinguish her from her sister) invited me to sit and rest my feet.

"I handle all the secretarial duties for Lord Leo. I live in the gate house with Mrs Quirk and her son Edward. He has freedom to roam about the property. You'll know him by his red hair and infectious smile, so just ignore him if you see him around the work areas. He's very friendly with all the men there after school. Sometimes he plays with Algernon, though we disapprove of such."

"Because he is not of the family?"

"No, because Algernon is a bad influence."

I went to supper with so many questions on my mind, the hermits and the Hedgehog, along with the Lady in White. Now I must add the curious Quirk sisters with a small fatherless boy. I determined to listen closely during these early days.

Within weeks of arrival, my first impressions held firm. The manor ran on a broken clock. One knew about when a meal or a tea would begin, but being on time was not a family trait. With the children under the care of the Scottish ladies, days could pass without my seeing them.

To my surprise, their parents seldom shared tea or supper as a couple. The reason was their very different interests.

Lord Leo was not quite lazy, more like a sea slug lumbering along the ocean floor. When he was not in his den reading, or in the trophy room with his Pudelpointer, he was on his favorite steed, Snotter. He prided himself on holding the best hunting ground in northwest Cornwall, miles of land unbroken by roads and rail ties.

One of Snerd's chores was to construct barriers that mimicked nature to provide jumps during the chase. He said Lord Leo was more excited by the regalia and thrill of the horse racing than the blooding of the fox. I were pleased to hear that, for Our Lord reminds us to take care of the smallest in the land, just as he takes care of the lilies of the field.

Betimes, his lordship went off to London, where the family kept a townhome. He said it were for business, but Jemima admitted it were to relax with his club friends there, many from his school days. It was called the Drones, and known more for its sporty men than for its politicians. I never knew such places existed, and prodded her to tell me all she could about them. It seemed near-sinful, a place of rich dinners and heavy drink.

Did I pass the Lord in a hallway, as expected I kept my eyes low. Nonetheless, I felt that bristle on the back of my neck that he was watching me. He never spoke, for even at fancy meals among friends he were a quiet man. I suspected he were not fully happy with his life.

Lady Gladys were the opposite. She talked with one of those brassy Yankee voices that pierced through thick walls. Fortunately, a bit of a hermit, she didn't often let out her tooty sound. Social events were the exception. And where Thelma Grubb had spent her mornings in bed reading her mail, Lady Gladys at dawn was in the kitchen grabbing fresh hot bread and cheese. Off she would go, on a hike, on side saddle, or in a carriage to a meeting somewhere. She often came back with something for one of her collections kept in a display room: a snakeskin, a badger skull, or a moth. Where another Lady might show off fine porcelain and small statuary, milady created a natural history museum.

Milady's latest endeavor was a refurbishing of the small separate chapel and manor graveyard. Church of England, it served the family and a few nearby gentry on Sundays, while servants like Alice and me went to the Slyme Gurney Chapel. I felt at home in the plain hall with its clear windows, its simple altar table and preacher's perch. The manor chapel, though, in the past had its walls white-washed to destroy earlier craven images. Despite removing remnants of the depraved Popish church, the visiting priest kept bits of its old ritual. Mrs Viscous said Lady Gladys was adding colorful hand-decorated cloths and new stained glass, more suggesting of High C of E. I had no notion the national church was really of two types, with one doing almost all but pray in Latin.

I wondered about the children, who saw their parents briefly each day, if at all. I were happy to be free of the Scottish ladies and their shushing ways! Mrs Viscous hinted at nasty stories about the two women, but I did not understand her disapproval. I would learn more than enough in time about the strange under life at Slanderley.

One morning I were outside beating small rugs, and arrived back at the trade entrance very disheveled, only to face an angry Mrs Quirk.

"Where have you been? You look a case for Dartmoor prison. I understand you are a good reader. Is that true?"

"Well, I did get prizes at school for my reading and writing. But I have not been able to keep up here, apart from studying the Bible afore bed."

"That will now change. Get yourself cleaned up at once and go to the library. His Lordship has hired a scholar to do some work in the archives, and he can use your help. You may skip afternoon duties from now on to work there. Not that you have spent heavily during those later hours!"

She turned in a huff, leaving me hang-jawed. Here I was all sweated out on her orders, yet she belittled me. Well, she was losing me part of the week now, so perhaps I took on the anger due someone else. I ran to the kitchen for some bread and butter, then did a quick wash before heading to the library.

I had never entered that room before, though I'd longed to see the books, maybe borrow one. I knocked before entering, opened the heavy oak door, and gasped at the vista before me.

Built in a corner of the manor, the space extended two stories, surrounded by shelves and drawers, with a second-story level reached by winding iron stair. It was darkened by heavy maroon drapes, to protect books from the sun, I guessed. Several higher narrow windows offered the little light, which explained the lamps on the tables and desks. Books and large boxes strewed over the surfaces.

Mr Bunston was in the room and introduced me. "This is Mr Norton, from Oxford. Since you are the one literate servant (his eyes rolling), we thought you could serve as assistant after luncheon."

The scholar emerged from a chair behind a wall of ancient bindings. His blond hair seemed green-toned, and he was tall enough to look me in the eyes. His smile disclosed large yellowy teeth, like organ keys. A spidery hand reached out. "Chippy Norton, archivist. Good to meet you. I need an all-sorts help here."

His grip was slippery.

"Well, sir, I have never even been inside this room. I welcome being at your service, sir."

"I appreciate your assistance in locating materials for me. I assume you can alphabetize and keep things in order. Once this is all cleaned up, you'll need to repair files and make new labels for everything. The old ones are unreadable."

His hands swept over piles of loose papers and books covered in dust on the work tables. Bunston said he would have tea sent over to us, that I was to start serious work the next day. He suggested we become better acquainted in the meantime.

Norton spoke first, as was natural in his superiority.

"My father and Lord Leo went to public school together and belong to Drones, where they meet up now and then. Pater happened to mention my history studies and love of archives, whereupon the Lord suggested I spend the next vac here. So here I am. And you?"

"I'm just a fisher's son, placed in service after me Tas and brothers died in a storm."

"So sorry about that," he said mechanically. "Though you are well-read, I hear. And feel free to call me Chippy. I'm not big on propriety."

"Thank you. Me Mam made sure of my schooling. I almost finished grammar school when the accident occurred. The village school were small yet had an excellent tutor, who lent me books as well."

"I hope we will get along. I fear most of your work will be physical. I do not handle heights well, and expect you will be up and down the ladders getting and replacing volumes. My particular interest will be the earliest documents, written in a script you will not be able to read."

He weren't the only one to have difficulty with heights, but I best not confess.

"I imagine you will dine with the family," I asked.

"Not at all. I have been granted the use of the old stone cottage on Gooseliver Creek. It is the oldest building on the estate and upgraded into a two-bedroom cottage. I understand a certain Mughatch will deliver my meals."

"Mug*watch*, the footman."

"Ah, yes."

He ate with a rare delicacy, as though each mouthful were precious, and often tipped his napkin to his mouth. I had to remind myself not to gulp everything quickly, a habit caught from the servant dining room.

"Tell me more," he inquired. "What do you do in your free time?"

"I'm sorry, sir, but there is not much. I have Sunday after Chapel. I read on stormy days, and hike on clear ones."

"Oh, do you happen to watch birds? I plan to find some new ones for my list. Living inland, I am unfamiliar with the sea birds."

I was beginning to wonder about the sanity of this lad. Watch birds? Keep a list? Birds to me were the gulls that tried to steal the fish I was sorting during childhood. Was I the first servant he ever spoke to for any length of time?

"Sorry, I have never had time to study nature. If you go left when the path back to the house splits, you can go down to the cove. There are often birds on the water there or overhead."

"Jolly good," he replied. "I'll see you tomorrow afternoon then. But before then, please read these notes on the history of the family, so you start with some understanding.

The Notes, of an unknown author follow here:

Abbott Cleese of Bungay Polytechnic, a fearless archive diver, traced the earliest documents. He discovered the original land assignment went back to James I, son of whorish Mary of Scots. The king granted the holding as a reward to his a favorite Protestant poet, Ismail Treconthick. Ismail's best known poem was "Ode to a Witch's Stake Long Burning." Ismail's descendants expanded the house, the acreage as well, thanks to their involvement in tin mines. As Cleese observed:

> *The Treconthick line died out, possibly as a result of grandson Launcelot's syphilis. A male cousin inherited but died without issue. He was gathering sea shells on the beach when an earthquake in Lisbon caused the great tsunami of 1755 that devastated Cornwall.*

Cleese gave up further research because the property went through the corrupt English probate courts for decades while lawyers fattened on the proceedings.

Enter the de Loverlys. Their origin remained unknown until a scruffy Christ Church Oxford student, Eligaynt Ewart, was rummaging in some dusty closet when he came across the following written by the college's 1830s Master:

"I don't know what we're coming to. I've given studentships to my sons, and to my nephews, and to my nephew's children, and there are no more of my family left. I shall have to give them by merit one of these days."

"Eureka!" Ewart shouted. "I finally have a thesis. I shall apply this model to other professions and establish myself." He did so, first through an analysis of Cambridge entomologists, to prove why none of them were studying ear worms. Deafness ran within the family that cluttered that generation of Dons, so the worms didn't infect them.

Ewart's amazing result led to his joining the haloed circle of Dons at Magdalen (Maudlin), where his father also taught. There he trained a generation of "Ewart Thesis" followers, who dove joyously into bottomless cruddy pits of documents to prove corruption. Somehow no one at Oxford ever pointed to the longstanding word, *nepotism,* well-known since the Medieval Ages. So much for Ewart Thesis originality.

A Magdalen student from Devon chose lawyers as his thesis topic, thanks to a lead from Dickens. ("The one great principle of English law is to make business for itself."} He happened upon the long-forgotten Slanderley case papers, which proved the family was the creation of a Judge Hugh Puissant Smurg, who finagled false papers with help of a forger pal. These placed the inheritance into the lap a Phineas de Loverly, by chance the newly chosen name of the Judge's youngest son.

At the time of settlement, the house was a shambles and tenant farmers growing only for themselves. It was like sending the lad to Yorkshire moors, but better than a youngest son could expect.

While working through dirt and cobwebs, Phineas came upon a cubby entered from a hidden staircase in what seemed to be the den. Inside were a bounty of riches. Some frugal Treconthicks had saved for a rainy day.

Set on getting a title, Phineas added wings, hired servants and grounds men, and created the current estate. While other Cornwalligans suffered from the collapse of tin mining, the de Loverlys rose to the top of the northwest duchy elite.

If you be confused, reader, join me. At least we can see how the de Loverly family were not real aristocrats. Still, they played a good game.

The Slanderley Curse

Calm Afore the Storm

Gleeves proved right. My new position went smoothest, so I lost all worries about life in Slanderley. I didna worry about Lady Gladys asking me to her chambers, nor of anyone amidst the servants like Squimm to taunt me.

My only unhappiness concerned my family, so far away, and not seen in two years. Although I had received letters from Mam, written by Mr Creakle or the minister, they were not enough. She seemed happy, and often spoke about me sisters' children. She assured me the fishing was fine as well. Still, her stories did not leave me content, for I knew she wanted me free of troubled thoughts. I did the same in my letters to her.

Because I were experienced, I did my daily chores quickly and took pride in the perfection of a polished boot or well-shined silver bowl. When supplies were needed from Bude, Gleeves took me in the carriage to the shops, where I handled the orders. Later years, I learned how my time there was most unusual, that most estates ran under a rigid rule of servant titles and chores. But Cornwall has always prided itself in going its own way. Slanderley was just more extreme and loose.

Under the quilt on my cumfy cot, I imagined the distant lands described in schoolbook poetry. Nights clamped me down like an anchor. A shout of "Fire" could not stir me up. Sometimes it is good to feel a prisoner, one's frozen body setting the mind off to visit imaginary realms.

One night I was more fretting than imagining myself in a distant land. That day, when a local tinkerer was enjoying cheese and bread in the kitchen, I overheard him chatter the latest news with Mrs Viscous. He said the fishing villages around Penzance were most troubled. The major harvest, of pilchards, was dire. The next harvest, of hake and such, did not make up the loss because French boats of the latest advance were sucking up the bottoms with their big maws. This was the third year of decline, he added. What terrible fate for Mousehole, especially for my brothers Goron and Conan. It was as if they were now swallowed by a large fish, not netting for one. Their new poverty meant no hope of weddings soon with their sweethearts.

Why had no letters from home mentioned this tragic change? Perhaps my family had been protecting me. Considering such, I grew angry. I were near a full-grown man, no more the baby. Were they true with me, I'd sent down some of my savings. I could still, but decided not. I sensed a power surging up my spine, a freeing from past hopes and family rule.

This awareness were just the hatch of an egg. I may be a man in body, but had yet to fit fully. I recalled a word from school, Corporeal. Substance. An adult male had substance. "There is life and food for future words," wrote Wordsworth, musing on his "thoughtless youth."

In the silent dark I ran my hands over my body, the rough carpet of late afternoon on my cheeks, the curls at the back of my neck, the sinews of my good-sized arms, the sweating pelt on my chest. My belly was firm, my manhood full-grown under bushiness. That act led me to the Biblical sin of Onan, and wandering hands left me in shame. To avoid that failing, on pleasant nights I went outside to walk off my evil impulses toward my private parts.

One such night, I leapt from my cot, desirous to walk under the swelling moon. I went down to the lake and followed the path by the follies, those odd little buildings of little use. Fish splashed, setting circles on the glassy surface. I took the path past the Pyramid to the Hedgehog. I stopped suddenly upon seeing its eyes were lit, from some interior source, and the nostrils were leaking smoke of a strange odor. Hadn't Snerd told me the building was shut up? Sneaking alongside, I heard nothing, for its shell was too thick to reveal any noises made inside.

Anyone returning from the reviled folly to the manor must pass by the Summer House. I picked a well-shadowed chair from which I could spy the path. Alas, I fell asleep following a long fruitless watch, and awoke after dawn, late for my morning duties.

Truth is, I was finding the work too easy, and at times went to the works area to see whether I could help Snerd or Sloth to offer assistance. One day I went out with Turgid to set rabbit traps for meat. On the way, he pointed out poacher traps, pits disguised by layers of leaves upon flimsy sticks. Along with Snerd, he taught me the ways of the wood, the means to survive off the rich wildness now ignored in this time of so many new inventions.

Despite his reptilian appearance, Chippy seemed a decent fellow. One afternoon he told me to take an hour to poke about and find all the locations of old deeds, letters, diaries, photographs, and such, what he called *ephemera*. Then he had me settle down by him to explain one of his problems. The archives were tossed into boxes without any method, so I understood why he was hired to organize the material.

When tea arrived, he called me over and began a conversation.

"It concerns a Curse. Can you imagine that? Involving a nun."

"That's interesting. I thought I saw a nun—"

"A nun long deceased. It's a taboo story around here, fingers crossed against future disaster. I suppose you haven't heard."

"Well, the carriage driver, Mr Gleeves—"

"Slanderley has a foggy history.

"I can see it from your Note—"

"Consider the murder of Randall by his wife in Italy. She's the one in the portrait at the top of the stairs.

"Yes, Mrs Quirk said—"

"Terrible slow death by poison. And then she had the audacity to move here and claim her widow's due."

"That is all new—"

"At least she got her just desserts."

"I didna—"

"Or Lady Peony, who died of a strange cloven-hoof disease."

"Tragedies repeat in some families. The Curse—"

"While *I* may not believe, nor *you,* the family and local people do. Just thought I'd alert you in case you run across the story in the pub."

"I don't—"

"Now, find me the files on Lady Euphoria."

"I'm sorry. Who is she?"

"She is Leo's much older sister. After Lady Peony's sudden death, she became like his mother. He sometimes calls her 'Nan,' in case you hear that name in conversation. I expect you'll find some boxes lying around with her name on them. Spread the documents out on that corner table and see if you can put them into categories."

I soon located two dusty green boxes filled with letters and drawings. I gathered the best approach would be to arrange everything by category and dates. It would be like solving a puzzle, except I was unable to read the handwritings well. I didna care, because these were private concerns, not of my due.

That evening, I reflected on Chippy's tale of a curse in light of Snerd's separate one. The past deaths of people in the Water Mill. Odd deaths of family members. A murder. Then I considered the stranger in the locked Hedgehog, the fleeting nun in the Summer House. I felt myself dropped into a mystery written by Mr Collins.

The weeks following held no surprises, and work turned me mind from foolish thoughts. One section of the library held all the best of the country's literature. I found novels Mr Creakle had described, often concerning the trials of the poor and the meanness of employers. I were almost afraid to handle the volumes, leather-bound with gilt decoration and frail pages protecting the illustrations. Chippy said Lord Leo was the only family member to take books from the library, that he was quite the literary sort. He allowed Eddie Quirk to borrow from the library as well, so I should not block the lad from doing so.

One evening, Mugwatch alerted me to a new opportunity, the first formal dinner since I arrived. He explained we would be serving under Mr Bunston's guidance. I tried on my uniform, which fit snuggly, for I must have gained more under Mrs Viscous's full belly meals. I confessed to him I had never served before. He had Mugwatch teach me typical place settings and the implements for particular courses. I were much grateful for his direction.

The afternoon of the dinner, Mrs Quirk called us in to alert us to the guests: the Bishop Wurzel and his wife Fanny, the Grimaces and their daughter from Bude, and the three spinster Tronek sisters. Lord Rashcum had to decline, which pleased staff, because he sometimes drank himself to sleep, his face drowning in the pudding.

We had to locate an extra-large chair for Fanny Wurzel, a great talker and eater, Mugwatch noted, so whoever served her must keep alert to refill her plates. Mugwatch gave me a rule to measure each item, while he made special folds on the napkins.

"Bunston does want a perfect table," Mrs Quirk advised. She then took us to the special pantry to unlock cabinets filled with the finest china and crystal. The plate decorations included the family crest along with an array of Lady Gladys's beetles, her favorite table-setting addition. We spent much of the afternoon placing everything on the table and in the service area. Meanwhile, Mr Bunston was in the drawing room arranging the drinks service. When he arrived to check our work, he breathed a heavy scent of gin over us. Being in his cups, he had to peer closely at the table and almost fell into one setting before approving the layout.

Because Lady Gladys arranged the menu, we found some unexpected choices. For some reason, it was all fish-based. The starter was a shellfish bisque. Other dishes included mussels, lobster *au gratin*, filets in some thick sauce, and a pudding stuffed with tiny shrimp. The menus were handwritten in French by milady herself, so I am only guessing the food. (Since you may know more, I put in that *au gratin* from her menu.)

Lord Leo was a full bred Cornwallegian and preferred his fish simple or coddled in a pasty bunting. I knew he must be cursing silently while poking at all the overly-buttered sea creatures. I agreed, for little is better than a juicy fillet fresh from the salty sea.

On top of that, Lady Gladys followed the American practice of eating very quickly, which cut down on much conversation. Not that it would have mattered. The speakers are incidental.

"Good weather."

"Mmph."

"Off to city soon?"

"Ahem, mebbe."

"Need rain."

"How's Jellicoe doing?"

"Mmph."

In the midst of this enlightening discussion, Bishop Wurzel's wife gagged on her overlarge fish portion. Mugwatch and I stood paralyzed, the guests similar in their seats, while she turned lobster red and stopped breathing. Then she fainted to the floor! Without thinking, I ran over and smacked her back hard with the side of my hand, as I was taught to unjam fish bones.

It seemed a miracle she hadn't died. Mugwatch and I helped her up to her seat, while she waved her hand over her face and apologized for upsetting everyone. Lady Gladys made a noisy show of digging into her meal, and everyone followed.

The dinner passed without further interruption, while I thought about the Curse.

More Intrigue

Word came one day that I must see Lord Leo in his trophy room. Apparently it was off the maid's cleaning list, for I coughed without break upon entering. Furry and hairy body parts connected by cobwebs to one another, while the cabinets shimmered in a snowy dust. Holding in a sneezing blast, I snuffled out my nose and tears ran down my face. Lord Leo ignored my outbursts.

"Harrumph, good job with Mrs, you-know, the other night, the Bishop's wife, Gundry."

"Thank you, sir.'

"I give no thanks," he suddenly blustered. "You were out of place! Next time, stand still and leave it to Bunston."

"Sorry, sir, but Mr Bunston seemed frozen in place."

"So he was. But rank must be observed. Do you understand me?"

"Yes, sir. I promise to defer in the future." *Defer* was a new word for me, which I at times confused with another one, *demur*. As you can see, language drifted up from my childhood schooling during these years of service.

Waving me away, milord turned to his latest "Horse Gazette." I wondered about his order, whether he'd have preferred the Bishop's wife to die, for she would have without my intervention. Whatever, I better understood his narrow views.

Since Norton didn't need me that afternoon, I had time for a short hike in solitude. With the aid of a stick, I stumbled down the snaky gravelly path to the cove to embrace the heartbeat of the surf. Perhaps the water would be calm enough for a short row, but I found the boat needed repair and carried only one oar. I reminded myself to alert Snerd to this problem.

Instead, I sat upon the upturned hull and watched the clouds piling up in the distance. I thought about the many vessels that lie in graves in the nearby sea, one of the most treacherous along Cornwall. No wonder local people imagined flickering blue lights on their chimneys to be ghosts of the drowned. I said a few prayers for their salvation and stood to leave, when a sudden clash caused me privates to contract.

The noise came from the old fishing cottage behind where Snerd and I had hid during the party. Peeping in the window, I saw little Algernon banging a chair on the ground, breaking it up into jagged sticks. His nurse not in sight, I went inside to stop him.

To my shock, he was crashing the chair atop a kitten, which by now was dead. I grabbed him and pulled him away.

"What's this? Where's Nurse?"

"Ha, I ran away from her."

"Why did you hit the kit?"

"I hate it. It's ugly, all black."

"You killed it! Now you must bury it!" I lifted the bloody body and put it on a cushion. "Here, carry this and come with me."

"It's just a stupid cat."

"No creature is stupid. You be bad! Let's find Mrs McCrae."

Holding the scruff of his shirt, I pulled him up to the house, where we found his nurse on the cliff edge calling for him. When I reviewed what happened, she thanked me and said she would take over.

I remained a bit in shock over what happened. Such a young lad, and so much evil. I knew the Scottish ladies taught him the straightway and would punish him severely. Yet, it were so worrisome that I went to see Mrs Viscous to describe the incident.

"I'm sorry to learn that," she responded. "This is not the first time the lad has behaved so. Before you came, Mugwatch found him throwing heavy rocks on frogs in the creek. He got some bad seed, that one."

"Do you mean The Curse?"

"No, nothing so silly. I don't believe in such tattle. It is just in the family, the American grandmother and mother. They brought the nasty blood. Colonials, bah!" She spit in her hand in exclamation.

Stunned by her reaction, I had to respond. "Lady Gladys seems normal. I mean I don't see her much, but she is always so well-dressed and polite."

"Oh, she's a sly one. She has secrets, I'm sure. Lady Peony, Lord Leo's mother, wandered off for weeks and returned to tell the strangest stories. Then there's the time she brought a sheep to dinner and claimed it was the reborn Lord Randall. Poor thing. She died suddenly, blood spilling everywhere. At least Leo and Euphoria were not tainted."

"What about Euphoria? Norton has me organizing her papers. Can you tell me about her? It will help my work with him."

"She's an artist and lives in the Mayfair townhouse when not off travelling about the Continent. Lady Peony left her a large inheritance, so she never had need to marry. She'll show up one of these days. The house is always brighter when she walks in. She sparkles like a shell fresh ashore."

Some days later, while helping Snerd repair and repaint the row boat, I described young Algernon's cruelty. Snerd told of a similar encounter, this one involving a pet mouse with its tail cut off. Cursed or by American blood, the de Loverly kin were hardly normal.

We had an early winter with "the fiercest storms in years," so said the locals. The rare winter sun was even less so, the normal heavy rains more a Noah's deluge. The chimneys screamed like banshees. Forced indoors, some Sundays we servants were unable to head out to Chapel. By January, family members and servants apiece found some place in the manor to cocoon away from others.

With Chippy Norton returned to Oxford, I still went to the library when I was free of house duties and continued to make up labels. I were never handy with a pen, so it was good practice to redo ones I had done poorly the previous summer.

Letty wandered in one afternoon with a large pad of paper and a watercolor set.

"I'm going to paint here," she announced. "Nurse is having one of those days."

"Perhaps that desk will serve you best. I'll light you a lamp. What are you painting?"

"Oh, nothing much. I hate painting! I hate stitching! I wish I could be outside." She slammed her pad on the table and walked over to me. "I would paint a horse, but I don't know how."

"I could find you a book with horses. Would that help?"

"Maybe, but really I just want to be away from everyone. Algie is always playing pranks on me, and Nurse wants me to behave more ladylike."

"Well, I understand that very well. Though no one here is nasty to me, I sometimes also want to be away from everyone. I think some of us are made that way. Such as your father."

She looked up at me with a wry smile. "So am I no one?"

"You are most welcome, my lady. You are not among those I wish to escape."

"I have a secret. You must not tell anyone. Cross your heart to promise!"

I did so without speaking, and knelt down to her level.

"I am getting a pony for my birthday! I heard my daddy tell my mommy."

"Well, that is nice, but it won't be a surprise now that you have heard about it."

"I don't care. I can pretend. Everyone pretends, you know."

"Are you sure? I think most people are truthful."

"Oh, no, not here. People here tell stories. You'll see."

"I must say I hope you are wrong. If they tell stories, how do you know you really will get a pony?"

"Because Mr Sexsmith came to visit. He knows all about horses and ponies so my pater is always consulting him. What was your pony like?"

"I never had a pony. I come from the seaside. We had cats to kill the mice."

"Aw, you can't ride a cat. Every child gets a pony. You must have had a mean mommy and daddy."

"Not at all," I laughed. "They were very kind, especially my Mam. I miss her very much."

Letty chewed her cheek in thought, then suddenly said, "Well, I need to be alone now to paint."

"I thought you didn't want to."

"Maybe you can bring me some horse books after all."

I found an ancient guide, *The Young Lady's Equestrian Manual*, along with a volume of horse sketches.

After setting her up, I went back to my work. She bent over the books for a while, then opened her art pad. She worked furiously with her pencil, sometimes erasing just as furiously.

The time passed quickly, the only sounds of our small instruments at work.

Letty suddenly rose and yawned. "May I see you again? The next time I sneak away from Nurse?"

"Please do, and tell me more secrets." I crossed my heart again.

Later I wondered about her belief that Slanderley people lied or made up stories. How could one so young and innocent come to such a conclusion?

Gratefully, the winter faded faster than usual, and as predicted, a young Welsh cob showed up for Letty's birthday, one that would grow along with her. Delighted by its sweet personality, she was out every morning before tutoring. As the days lengthened, she fled the house to ride a second time. Apart from rainy days, she stopped coming to the library.

"She's a natural," noted Snerd. "She has no fear and will be on a full horse as soon as she is large enough."

"She must get it from her father," I suggested. "He looks happiest when he is out on Snotter."

"Aye, and pray the Curse don't lead him to have a bad accident. He charges barriers and fences others would avoid. He can be ruthless with an animal, and has lost two already with his hard pressing. Some people will no longer sell him a steed—they think him close to cruel."

I demurred. "You are telling tales, Snerd. I have never found Lord Leo any other than gentle and calm."

"Despite your large size, you are still a lad, Kenal. Fisher boys don't learn much of the real world."

What is this? Twice in a week I am told, dare I say, that I'm childish in my thinking. I knew from books I read that life is full of puzzles and nasty people. Mr Dickens taught me well there. But it was his job to tell stories. Surely the daily life of people were not so complicated and full of deceit.

That spring, the house awoke along with the fluttering bluebells. Mrs Quirk called both inside and outside staff together one evening to go over upcoming plans. Not only would there be a formal dinner with guests at least once a week, but Lord Leo was interested in a long weekend party as well. Weekend guests would bring personal servants as well, so we must prepare for crowded service rooms, with extra cots added where possible. That was for later in the summer, we heard with relief.

Now Lord Leo and Lady Gladys met more often to dine together. She seemed perkier and pinker than in recent months, and much more talkative. She dominated the conversation, while his Lordship nodded distractedly. She jabbered about the newest sheep, Algie's next birthday, rumors about the King's mistresses, and complaints about the Scottish Nurses.

The only time Lord Leo seemed to pay attention was when she discussed her latest plans for the family's private church. It stood alone, one of the few structures in original state. Unused for decades, its neglect deserved attention. But Lady Gladys was thinking such ritual additions as an eternal light hanging above the altar, which she had already fancied up with colorful cloths.

On Sundays, the family often went to St. Olaf's in Poughill, which Lord Leo preferred for its 14th century dour atmosphere. Afterwards, they met their town friends, the simpering Tronek sisters or the well-named Grimaces. It was around this time that Lady

Gladys became enamored of a service even further south, St Werburgha in Warbstow. That modest chapel was dedicated to an Anglo-Saxon nun.

I didna hold to saints in Chapel, certainly not of holy women living in a kind of coven without men. Give me a plain church, plain talk, and plain Scripture. The Bible is enough, no need for the mumbo-jumbo.

Anyway, back to the happy spring. One reason for the new joyous atmosphere was the arrival of Lord Leo's sister, Euphoria. She arrived in late March, the carriage filled with baggage, paintings, and sculpture, much of her own making. Taller than her much-younger brother, her profile revealed a lantern chin and thick black tresses wound up on top of her head. She wore a cape like Joseph's coat of many colors. Unlike the Lord and Lady, she was lively and always smiling.

Letitia dashed out of the house to greet her.

"Auntie Eu, you are back! I have missed you so much," she said, spreading her arms wide for a hug.

"My, you're grown so much taller. I think you will be like me when you grow up."

"I hope so! Will you teach me to dance? I hear there are new dances in the city. And guess, what—I have a pony! You can come riding with me."

"Now, Letty, you know I am not much for horses, but I promise to sit at the Summer House and watch you prancing in the meadow and around the lake. What's its name? He has a lovely pied coat."

"Bruckle, because he likes to splash in the creek" replied Letty.

A shouting Scottish burr broke in. "Miss Letitia! Leave your aunt alone and get dressed for dinner!"

The visitor turned to me, still holding the door. Her eyes almost met eye level.

"Well, and you are?"

"Kenal, ma'am."

"It's nice to see some fresh blood. Please take my cases up to the Gherkin suite in the East Wing, but leave my easel in the small room next to Lord Leo's den. The large wooden box holds my paints, so that goes there as well."

"Yes, ma'am. My pleasure, ma'am."

"Oh, don't 'ma'am' me like an old lady. I don't stand on such formalities. Now, where is my brother?"

She took her carpet bag from the carriage seat and swished up to the house, a rainbow breaking the gloomy façade.

One of Euphoria's first decisions was to send Letty's Scottish Nurse packing. It took little to convince Lord Leo.

"The girl is too old to be stuck in the nursery with her brother. He still needs watching and training, but in another year she can go to the local daily Lady School. Meanwhile, I'll introduce her to better books and drawing."

See what I mean? One less servant to pay, perfect for Lord Leo's tight fist.

She also moved Letty down from the nursery to the Prune Suite adjoining hers. That way they could breakfast together and Euphoria oversee morning lessons.

Serving dinner several evenings later, I was not surprised to find the girl seated at the table in a fluffy violet fancy dress. She was silent, though full of smiles while Euphoria recounted some of her escapades abroad.

"Really, Leo, you must go to the Continent one of these days. I can't believe you have never left England. Gladys, you did the Grand Tour, no?"

"Of course. It is a *rite de passage* for any well-bred young American woman. My brother Cornelius accompanied me. Oh, the Wiesbaden trout! The potatoes of Aix! The sausages of Rome! That is where I found my love of tomato beetles."

"But the architecture? The Nile? The museums?"

"*Mais non.* I could not enter *habitations* with images of *les nuditées.*

"Forgive me, Gladys. I have overlooked your Puritan country's protectiveness of its young women. Perhaps you will join me one day and I can treat you to the greatest masterpieces. Surely you are now old enough to visit the Louvre and the Pergamum."

"*Mais non, merci.* Now that I am wed, I have seen enough of *les nuditees.*"

Lord Leo interrupted. "Now, Nan, no need to pressure Gladys." He pressed his wife's hand. "She's perfectly happy in our secluded hideaway, are you not, my dear?"

"I am even more now that I have found those who share my deep Christian beliefs." She slipped her hand from under his.

"You mean those incense-stinking rituals and flagellations. So long as you keep me out of it," he grumbled.

"Leo, it is just a *petite* hobby of mine. I do appreciate your allowing me such."

"So long as you don't join a nunnery."

Though everything was stated politely, I heard the undercurrent of a major disagreement. Unlike other lords of the manor, Leo was constrained somewhat by the fact it was Gladys's money that refurbished Slanderley and kept its stable full of the finest horses. Nor could he squash her updates of the family church. (Mrs Viscous believed that clauses in the American wedding contract ensured Gladys's relative freedom.)

Euphoria broke the resulting uncomfortable silence.

"I am thinking we need a May fete for our neighbors and tenants. What do you think, Letty? Would you like to help me with the planning? It would be like a parish fair, but much livelier and fun. You can find some ponies to borrow for children to ride."

Lord Leo dug into his pudding. "That will take quite an outlay, not sure we can supply," he mumbled.

"I am happy to contribute from my private funds," assured Lady Gladys. "I have heard so much about these fetes, yet never attended one."

"Well, that's settled," Euphoria concluded. We shall have a May Pole and folk dancers and a tent full of Cornish specialties.

Letty clapped her hands excitedly. "Oh, Auntie, it will be so nice to see visitors my age. The only people who come here are the Bishop and his wife, or riders for the hunts. A May Pole sounds lovely. We will need lots and lots of ribbons. What colors?"

"You shall start by making a list of the children you would like to invite. Of course, the tenant children will come too."

"There are the Elmsby sisters and their cousin Phillip. Although he's older, Reggie from Cromwoh would fill in another boy. He loves horses as much as me."

"As much as *I*. The *do* is implied."

"Yes, Aunty. As much as I."

At bedtime, I alerted Mugwatch to the plans. We hoped we would not have to do any heavy work—the tents and the ribboned pole, for example. I had hoped to build a friendship with him, but when in our shared room he be closed as a clam. He were not interested in the novels and poetry books, even when I offered to read aloud. He didna go to Sunday Chapel with me and the others either. I suspected he be a secret Roman Catholic, for his hands were often moving under his blanket, fingering a rosary no doubt.

Despite my failure in finding fellowship with Mugwatch, I made friendships with others. Mrs Viscous talked to me like a kindly aunt, ready to listen to my rare troubles and suggest ways to solve problems. Snerd and Sloth were nae men for Scripture nor Chapel, yet I found them good men. I regretted the likelihood they faced no Salvation. I knew they liked to tease me in a fun way, which I took as their show of affection.

My favourite of all in service was Alice, the top maid. When I could, I sat beside her at table. She were some years older than me, so I adopted as an older sister. Without saying such, she seemed to understand my view toward her. She were slim with long wheat-colored hair she kept in a tight roll for work. I saw its full glory once when she was in a back field after washing it. She lay on the warm grass with her hair spread behind her like a fan to dry and bleach in the sun.

She were taller than me as well, yet took my arm on the rocky trail to Sunday Chapel. She'd little schooling, and enjoyed the rare times I could read to her from the Bible, mostly Psalms, no Lamentations. She were also my main source of information about life above the stairs. Here, an example of our talk.

"Lady Gladys seems strange to me. She skulks around and likes to hide in the Summer House when she is not off on a ride."

"Kenal, what you say is true, but I don't think she is strange. I think she is confused by our customs. She has been lonely as well. You had to move from home, so you should understand the difficulties."

"But she is the lady of the manor. She can have anything she wants. She brought money with her as well."

"She was not trained for her role. She has told me of what her life would have been had she married an American. Wealthy women there have become emancipated. Some even talk of the vote, if you can imagine. They have their own clubs and a few have divorced. Also, she was used to the rich social whirls of New York and Newport. Oh, the balls she has described to me!"

"Still, she came here. That were a choice."

"Kenal, she came only to save her favourite sister from being sent. Unlike her sister, she saw no possible suitors among their friends, and was not sure she ever wanted to marry. She said she always preferred the company of women. It is women she sees at the Summer House."

I were not convinced, but I looked at milady with a kindlier eye after that conversation.

The Slanderley Curse

Disappearance

It were such a bounteous spring that I near forgot about me poor family and the fishless sea. Any flowering plant burst twice as large as last year, while the hens laid eggs the size of ostriches. Honey tasted like wine, not that I would know. The storms whispered rather than shrieked, so the Celtic Sea spit fewer dead seamen onto the shores.

The fete day approached, and I were relieved to be free of clearing and building. Rather, Snerd watched over the local workers brought in for the duty. They set up a tent to cover a buffet set with cakes, finger sandwiches, and drinks. The maypole was not too tall, just right for children to spin about with colorful ribbons. In addition to the bandstand was a small wooden deck for folk dancing. Small tables and chairs clustered for comfort. The local schoolmaster set up an area for races and games he would oversee.

Lady Gladys did not like to be in the sun, so a separate open tent with carpeting allowed her friends to join her in shade. It was my job to serve there, while Mugwatch and Alice served in the general buffet tent.

The afternoon were warm, with just enough breeze to cool those out in the sun. Standing at the edge of Lady Gladys's tent, I enjoyed the small band play for the folk dancers and the May Pole twirlers. Some village men sang mournful sea chanteys with a rich blend so intense that noisy talkers stopped to listen. The men's final song was the famous madrigal about five fathoms down, the dead with pearls for eyes. It were the one sad moment the entire afternoon.

By sunset, Lord Leo's face was beetroot from tromping about the meadow and copse with his friends, while Lady Gladys remained pale, as did her companions. The tenant children left with paper cones filled with candy, while their parents staggered under weight of all the food and ale in their bellies.

When all left my tent, Mrs Quirk told me to use a mule cart to take all the settings and linens back to the house in one move. For once all was in the scullery for others to clean, so I was free for the night. I planned to gorge on leftovers brought from the buffet tent. Alice greeted me in the kitchen with a slice of Stargazy pie. She reminded me of my older sisters, always doing small kindnesses.

Content in her company, I suggested we take a sit on the cliff top during the few minutes of dusk left. We let Mrs Viscous know in case we were needed unexpectedly. Alice led the way to the old fallen tree trunk carved into a bench. We sat there long after sunset, the sea sounds soothing after a hard day. We discussed our pleasure that all had passed without incident. The mix of tenants and gentry fell into well-known patterns, each at their own activities and cordial in crossing.

"I'm pleased you invited me, Kenal. I have some news. I am thinking of leaving Slanderley."

"Oh, no—I should miss you dearly. You have been so nice to me and helped me out when troubled. Why would you go from this quiet spot?"

"It isn't certain, and I can't tell you why. I have had some botherings. You are too young for me to explain. Perhaps they will stop."

Botherings? Who would cause Alice such upset?

"So can I nae help?"

"Leave it to me, Kenal. I may be a woman, yet I am not all weakness nor frailty."

A thick fog was tiptoeing in on cats' paws, so we returned to quarters. I watched Alice head up the long stairs to the women's rooms in the attic. I had never been there, though heard they were cold and cramped, unlike the men's below. No wonder the maids kept fingers knitting shawls and mittens on free evenings.

I were so tired that I fell into bed and went fast asleep. I kept a candle on for Mugwatch, for his bed appeared empty.

The next morning I awoke refreshed, stretched, yawned, and dressed. Then I rushed to the kitchen, breathless, with good reason.

"Mugwatch is not in his cot. Have you seen him?" I asked Mrs Viscous.

"Nae, why would he be up this early? You are always the first down for a cup before you do the boots."

She was correct. Because I had the early duties, I normally crept about our room while he continued to sleep.

Nor did he come later for breakfast.

"Where could he be?" was the theme of the chatter.

Turgid added to the concern. "I'd not seen him this morning when I did my usual check about the sheds and stables. That's not surprising, for he seldom came into the work areas."

Mrs Quirk recalled, "I can't recall giving him final orders when the guests left. He must have taken the silver from the buffet tent into the butler's pantry, because it is all there waiting for Kenal to polish today."

"Perhaps he's taken off," said Snerd. "Ye know he's been talking about finding another placement, one closer to Plymouth where his family lives."

"Or he has simply saved his from his weekly dosh and planned to skip out all along," added Turgid.

I disagreed. "The problem with that possibility is his clothes and goods were in the room when I awoke. He wouldn't take off without them. The iron bank that held his savings is still on his table."

Mrs Viscous countered, "Well, he could have gone off for the night with a tenant girl. He might be staggering over from a barn right now. He is of the age to be tempted to do so."

"Mugwatch has always been true to his post," replied the scullery maid.

"He never slacks. I have always been able to count on him," agreed Mr Bunston.

Mrs Quirk said, "This talk is doing no good. Let us hope he is safe and well."

"Let us pray it be so," I murmured. "I wish I could say more, but he has always stayed to himself. He were not a gossipy sort either."

Alas, we rushed to our daily work. We had extra chores to handle the excess from the party. I faced extra dirty and grass-covered shoes and the extra silver tea sets to polish. The laundry woman, Tabitha, complained about all the hand scrub of the fancy dresses.

When Mugwatch failed to show up for midday meal, our worries gnawed. No one had come across sign of him during their various duties.

"We need to check the lake," advised Alice. "Maybe he went for a dip after work. It was such a warm, inviting evening. Maybe he drowned!"

"Or went down to the beach and got caught in the tide. You know how suddenly it can pull a wader down," remarked Turgid.

"Could this be the Curse?" Alice wondered. "Will we never find him?"

"Oh, that silly thing," said Tabitha. "That's just a Cornish tale. If you believe that, then I suggest a vampire came and sucked his blood. All we'll find is skin in a flat set of clothes."

"This is no time for jest," snapped Mrs Quirk. "We will have to do serious searching. After dinner the men can go out now into the woods, check the lake, the outbuildings, and the follies. We women will do the manor. For now, get back to your chores. We have wasted enough time. I am sure he took a scupper."

That afternoon I were in the library rearranging the geography books, when I heard loud murmurs, then a call, "He's been found!"

Following the direction of the shouts, I discovered both family members and servants in the front drive. Letty was there by her pony. Her face was white and messy with snot while she gasped for breath.

"Calm down, Letty. It has nothing to do with you," advised Lord Leo. "People do die."

Lady Gladys handed over a linen handkerchief. "Now clean yourself up and take Bruckle back to his stall."

Even Euphoria offered little comfort. Clapping her hands loudly, she barked, "Hurry up, Letty, it is almost time for your French lesson. Quit that sniveling."

"You men go and cover the body, while I call Mr Iliac and police," ordered Lord Leo. "It was surely an accident, but we must follow procedures."

The others led me down the lawn to the ha-ha. Apparently Letty had been riding alongside its boundary when she looked down to see the corpse at the deepest section. He lay like a fallen puppet, arms and legs oddly bent, his head lying with right ear on right shoulder. Worst of all, his eyes splayed open in astonishment.

"Looks like he's broken his neck," Turgid noted unnecessarily. "And his left leg as well."

"Poor lad," added Snerd. "Twere such a dark night. He must have forgotten about the ha-ha while he were out star gazing."

"It's no wonder we missed him, the ha-ha doing such a good job of making a clean stretch of meadow," I added. "Let me lead a prayer for his soul."

All bowed their heads while I repeated well-known phrases said over the dead. When I said Amen, most left to return to their duties. I started to clamber down into the ha-ha when an arm stopped me.

"Turgid and Sloth will cover the body and watch," said Snerd. "You go off to your duties. This is for us older men to handle. We must keep the area clean for the police to study."

I returned to the library, shaking in a kind of aftershock. Soon I heard arrivals, Mr Iliac and police, no doubt. Indeed, a burly constable came in the room to talk with me.

"This is just a formality, understand. I have to ask everyone whether they saw the victim the night of the fete. We just want to reconstruct when he had his accident. I understand he roomed with you."

"That evening I watched the sunset from the cliff with Alice. I was so tired from the day's duties, you see, so I barely said my prayers. Mugwatch wasn't abed yet, though I was not concerned. Unlike me, he tippled, and some nights stayed late with other men over a homemade brandy. I only noticed him missing the next morning."

"What was he like? Would anyone have a reason to harm him? addressed the constable."

"He were very quiet and did his work well. We had separate chores, so we did not see one another much during the day. He were friendly enough at mealtime. I canna imagine why another would harm him. Were it not an accident?" I noted.

"No reason to be suspicious or start a rumor. It was most certainly an accident, but we have protocol to follow," the constable stated firmly.

"He will be missed. I'm sorry I can't be more helpful. He worked most with Mr Bunston, who may be more helpful," added Mrs Viscous.

The butler, sober for once, affirmed the value of Mugwatch's labor.

"Thank you. We'll not bother you again." As the constable was leaving, he turned back. "Do you know anything about his family? We need to get in touch, for sending the remains, that is."

"Mrs Quirk will have all that information," explained Bunston.

Afterward, I thought what I had seen in the ha-ha. That head, so twisted in the ditch. The eyes wide open in surprise. I shivered at the recall.

Procedures followed more quickly. Mrs Quirk packed Mugwatch's clothes and few personal items to send off with his corpse to the village near Plymouth where he grew up. Lady Gladys arranged a fancy hearse carriage as a way of showing her sympathy to his family. Mr Bunston advised it might be some time before a replacement was hired, so I moved over to Mugwatch's better cot.

Within a week, all sign of the man was gone, his presence forgotten.

The Curse Revealed

Summer was a-coming in. I didn't miss Mugwatch in particular, though I did regret not having an extra hand when guests came for dinner. Though promoted to First Footman, I had almost double the work. I discovered Lord Leo used Mugwatch as a quasi-valet, less to dress and cater to his toilette than to keep his clothes brushed, cleaned, and sent off for any mending. Even though his lordship was not prissy about his appearance, nor a taskmaster, his chores left me less of the few free hours I valued.

In addition, Chippy Norton returned from Oxford, so I had my duties to him as well. One day I decided to speak up and went to the housekeeper's sitting room.

"Mrs Quirk, I take pride in my work. I do not slack. Currently though I am forced to neglect perfection in order to get all my chores done. Can we nae get a replacement for Mugwatch? I have too many masters: you, Mr Bunston, Lord Leo, and the librarian."

"I have spoken repeatedly with Mr Bunston about this, but you know his procrastination. Perhaps I can go around him and ask Jemima to place the position with an agency and prepare some interviews. It's clear Mr Bunston is not picking up the charge."

"If I dare suggest, perhaps advertise for a valet. Lord Leo mumbles he does not need such attention, though I am sure he would enjoy it. Mr Bunston can assign the other tasks Mugwatch handled, to assist at tea and drinks service, for example. Sorry if I seem beyond my place with this idea."

"No, Kenal. You make good sense. I will consult with his lordship and Jemima in regard to your proposal. It will of course be my idea."

Following this conversation, she said nothing, so I remained in the dark until a chance meeting with Jemima two weeks later.

"Kenal, we will be advertising for a Valet position. By rights we should offer it to you first, but you have just been promoted. Bunston and I will interview the candidates before referring the best to Lord Leo for approval. I trust this causes you no ill will."

"Not at all. I have my work with Mr Norton on top of everything else, and lack the experience to be a valet. So long as the person is of good humor, I welcome him, as will the others in service."

"Very good. While you are about, please take these books up to the family suite and leave them in the private sitting room. They have anxiously been waiting for them to arrive by post from the City."

While heading to the family apartments, I glanced at the titles: *The Moths of the British Isles* was for her ladyship, I suspected, to expand her knowledge of small creatures. *The Spectre of Tappington* was an old horror story I'd read at Pennididdle. *The Man Who Was Thursday* was a new novel by one G. K. Chesterton, an unfamiliar name. Who wanted these stories? *Plants Poisonous to Livestock* was for Lord Leo, to be certain his horses and cattle were safe from danger.

As I placed the books in an array on the desk, I heard shouting from one of the adjoining bedrooms. I could not ken the words clearly, yet the voices were of his lord and lady. I turned to leave without notice, when a loud crash preceded the appearance of Lady Gladys out the door. Seeing me, she grabbed my arm and pushed me with her into the hallway. I noticed some blood on her right hand, which was gripping a rosary.

"Milady, can I help you?"

She said nothing, but pulled me down the main staircase and into the nearest drawing room. There she finally spoke.

"I will be alright, Kenal. I am pleased you were there to see me out."

She let go of me and fanned herself while moving about in agitation.

"Please forget what just happened. My husband was having a terrible headache and took it out on me."

"But your hand—"

"Just a cut when I broke a glass. See, it is not much. I will go and wash it up now."

"I left your new books on the desk," I noted to change the topic. "I hope you enjoy them."

She stopped to face me with a weak smile of understanding, then went out of the room.

I realized my heart was pounding from this sudden, unnatural encounter. She had lied about the headache. She would not have rushed out from the argument so quickly were it not serious. Had Lord Leo threatened her?

Feeling frightened, I needed to talk with someone. Heading through the garden, I came upon Snerd and Turgid sitting on a bench facing the statue of Piraner, the drunken miner. Smoke casually drifted from their pipes as though they were men of freedom. Did they ever work?

"Ye look a bit persnickered," said Turgid. "Like ye had a scare."

"I did, of sorts, though I have promised secrecy to the one involved." I took a long breath to calm down. "Most days everything here is calm and smooth. Then something odd or scary happens. Mugwatch, for example."

"Aye, it's the Curse."

"No one has really explained it to me. Was there a curse, or is it just Cornish story-telling?"

Snerd slid over to make room. "Sit down beside us, and I will fill you in. I'm surprised the librarian hasn't told you."

"I know nae as well," said Turgid. "Just that people told me not to work here cause of the Curse."

Snerd refilled his pipe to prepare for a long tale.

"Twas a dark and stormy time, long past. I think it were when Sinjin was Lord. Have you heard of him, married to the crazed Lady Peony? Or were it Lord Philo? I'm not too sure."

"Does the time matter, Snerd? Just get on with it," whined Turgid.

"It must have been Philo, cause he had a brother named Albert who were the cause of all the troubles. Wookie Hole Caverns, I think."

"Where is that? I never heard of it. Is it nearby?" I asked.

"It's just a set of failed tin mine digs. The cave openings are large and cool, making for pleasant rooms on hot days. They are a good spot to rest with friends after being out on the moors. Or to avoid a sudden rain. I can show you one day."

"I'd like that, Snerd. Thank you."

"Speaking of which, do you know of the moor haunts? The devil, the dark dog, the fairies? Any one of them could turn you into a bramble bush or stone pillar. Being a fisher boy, they could make great play of your innocence."

"I know all about Piskies, Snerd. We had our own shrieking ladies near Lands End." I made a wide-eyed grimace and made high-pitched moans.

Turgid pressed on. "What about this Albert and the curse?"

"Being second son, he enjoyed a roaming eye. He be a very successful one with his curly locks like polished coal and lips like strawberries. Even the better ladies of the area welcomed his visits, for he were also a musician and poet, quick with words like tempting tongues. One he visited on his rounds was the abbess at Gimunderford-upon-Withover in Devon. Called St Vulva's Priory, I recall."

"I thought an abbess, being a nun, would not consort with a man."

"You are so naïve, Kenal. Even the most pious have impulses to sin. The abbess, Sister Labia, being of porcelain beauty, had entered the convent following a time of unsuccessful courtships. She finally convinced her father that she had always desired a life of prayer.

"At first, of course, Albert visited to ask for religious teachings. Eventually his conversations with Labia changed to more worldly matters. She was, being naïve and virginal, easy to woo."

"And no one noticed?"

"Remember, the abbess has private quarters. Labia was strict, though in a kindly way, so her charges admired her too much to assume any bad thoughts of her. That was, until she returned one day from an outing with Albert. She wrenched at her clothes and threw herself prostate on the altar aisle, where she remained all night in prayer. Nuns and novices could not get her to move. Days later, she sent Albert her curse:"

"What did she write?"

"I canna say. There may be a copy somewhere in the library. Words passed among the servants of the time claim Sister Labia was unhappy with Albert's actions concerning, you know what I mean."

I finally had some sense of what Snerd meant, if not in great detail. I could hardly control my disgust. His tale was a jest, a means to make fun of my Chapel background, my chastity.

"I am not so foolish to believe that, Snerd. I do not thank you." I stood to go away.

"Wait, before you rush off, think. What about the strange deaths and murders that have blemished this family? Why do so few people visit? Why be large social events so rare?"

I wondered about the nun I had glimpsed during my stay. Was she the ghost of Labia? Could the Curse be true? I left without a retort. Snerd's loud snickers followed me down the pathway.

There I were, a brawny lad in a kind of Bedlam. The lord would rather me let a guest choke to death than save her. The lady was known for strange ramblings and obsessions. The grounds man told stories of nasty doings that led to a Curse. The butler was a tippler, the cook, a gossip. An earlier family member had murdered her husband. My fellow footman had a terrible accident. So far, the only truly sane person seemed to be Alice, who led the pure and pious life of my leanings.

A returning Chippy Norton appeared in high spirits, and invited me to join him for sherry after our first day's work together in the library. I had warmed up to him the previous year, because he were patient with my faults. Nonetheless, I resisted his invitations to hike out and search for birds to admire.

"So, tell me all about the, ahem, unhappy event involving this Mugwatch."

"Broke his neck by falling into the ha-ha. What he was doing down the lawn in the middle of the night is a puzzle."

"Drink, no doubt."

"Could be. He did have friends in Slyme Gurney for such sinful imbibing."

"But wouldn't you know he had gone off? You shared a room."

"We were both worn to nibs from the May fete. Just collapsed in bed, I were, before him. When I awoke, he were gone. No one was more surprised than I."

"Feel guilty a bit?"

"Nae, what could I have done to prevent his foolishness? We all knew of the ha-ha's depth at that point. It were a dark and foggy night, though, so he could just have lost his sight. Alice and I had been sitting by the cliff edge, and finding our way into the manor was frightful."

"Or something might have distracted him while he walked."

"That makes the most sense, doesn't it? It's what most decided, though not everyone here. They point to the Curse, you know."

"Oh, that again. There is evidence for some eccentricities at the abbey involving Sister Labia. There are rumors of some document at Exeter Cathedral. Add on to that the circumstances of her lover Albert's death."

"What of his death?" This was becoming even more curious.

"One evening he failed to show up for a dinner at nearby Cromwoh. Since he had planned to stay overnight there, the Slanderley staff were unaware he had gone missing. A large cadre of constables and townsfolks searched the roads and both estates without finding sign of him. Several days later, alerted by a rank odor, a gardener discovered Albert inside the Pyramid, his body neatly dismembered. The hermit who had lived there was gone and never again seen. They learned later he'd originally trained as a butcher's apprentice. The family sealed the structure up tight with

Lord Albert's remains within. It didn't seem right to place him in hallowed ground."

"Sorry, Chippy, this is too much for me to take in. The Curse, the dead bodies. Do you even feel safe here?"

"Of course. There are logical explanations for everything. The Curse seems to make random coincidences appear otherwise. People feel safer as a result. Had nothing happened later to Albert or others at Slanderley, it would be long forgotten, a slip of paper in some Archive. Not that one exists. Wouldn't we have seen a copy by now?"

"I be of Chapel. I know nothing of the monks and nuns. Only that Henry forced them to close, and much later a few came back."

"Yes, Henry's squashing of the Roman church only sent its believers into the underground. New monasteries and convents emerged after the laws allowed such. They became very different, modest in size and lacking in wealth. In 1849, Lord Ffurze took over the habitable remains of an old Devon Abbey to create a place for private prayer. He learned that the Daughters of the Divine Maternity were looking to expand into a new convent and invited them in. Locals referred to it as the Uterine Priory, not St Vulva's."

"It doesn't sound like much praying went on to me. How did the Abbess become so sinful a woman?"

Chippy began to pace the room while giving forth his wisdom. I suppose that is how Oxford dons measured their thoughts during lectures. His voice changed to a rich baritone, better to appeal to the ear.

"What happened during Henry's time reoccurred. I have researched one nunnery in particular. The Oxford gentry who founded the Littlemore Priory provided buildings, land, and a collection of valuable furnishings. By the early 1500s, he ignored the women's needs, being certain that creating the religious community was sufficient to save his soul. That is, he quit offering any funds for upkeep. In time, the nuns had to pawn goods in order to eat. They shared beds after hawking most of the furniture.

"Now forward several hundred years. By the time Sister Labia became head of St Vulva's, she was at her wit's end. Lord Ffurze too failed to continue annual support. Then she recalled the Littlemore nuns, and decided to follow their lead. Her intent was to become pregnant by Albert and thus force him to become the new regular benefactor."

"You suggest she meant well? She sinned in the worst way! Surely she could have found other pious supporters."

"I could tell you more about her neglected upbringing and offer that as an excuse, but I think we are missing the point. Littlemore was a rare occurrence that Henry VIII used as propaganda to describe all religious orders. A few sources suggest Sister Labia was a bit deranged and accustomed to buying curses from the local travelers. She believed in spiritual nonsense along with her traditional beliefs. As do too many folk around Slyme Gurney and Slanderley. Just unreliable word of mouth, gossip."

"So you think all the murders were—"

"Just coincidence. Yes."

"And you are not afraid to stay here?"

"Not at all. Can you believe Albert would fail to please Sister Labia?"

So there was Chippy Norton, full of rationality, while on the other side was Snerd, wary about unseen threats. Where did I stand? Confused.

I would like to say Lady Gladys called on me again following that strange encounter outside her suite. Twas not to be so. Indeed, the next time I served the family, Milord and milady virtually billed and cooed while feeding one another. I bit my tongue not to laugh aloud. Later I wondered whether they were trying to make me do so. Or drive me mad.

"Dearest Bunny," he peeped. "I think it is time for a long weekend with guests." He popped a slice of his pasty in her mouth.

"Really, Puss? When? Who should we invite?" She spread open her mouth like a newborn fledgling.

"I am thinking harvest time. None of the outlying gentry want to be home when the fields are being cleared. Someone always gets killed, and you know what a bloody mess that can be. Remember when Nettle was impaled on a rake? No, you wouldn't. You were off somewhere on a pilgrimage. I don't remember either, being off to the Drones. But Jemima described it all in horrid detail. The thoughtlessness of the farm workers. Bleeding into the crop." He fed her a tiny bit of swede.

"Don't say more. You know how I hate bodily fluids. At least Christ arrives in the form of bread and wine, not a bit of liver or toe." She forked a slip of bread into his mouth.

"Sorry, Bunny. I say no more of that nasty intrusion. I was thinking we could invite people in the guise of celebrating the purchase of Golgotha."

Golgotha was a new prize steer, bought at auction to breed a bulkier sort of beef cattle. He had just arrived. Upon checking him out, Turgid doubted it were much interested in mating with the female of its species. "Even animals can be twisted," he snickered. "Be poofs, in case you don't get my meaning."

What was this bit about poofs? People spoke of them as though I understood. Twas not a word I learned in Mousehole. Whatever, I gathered it were horrific, a nasty disease, perhaps? I pretended not to hear. Me mam taught me not to snigger at others, to join in unkind tattle. Nonetheless, I hoped I were not in danger of being a poof. I admit to wanting to be liked.

Throughout the conversation, Euphoria ate quietly while attempting to hold back her own snigger. Back to the dinner conversation, as I recall.

Lady Gladys continued. "I know you love Golgotha, my Pussywussy. Yet not everyone is into well-hung bulls. Me, for example. Can you think of something else to fill the weekend?"

"Of, course, my Fuzzy Bunny." He munched a long time on a mutton chop. "I've got it! We can make it an auto event. Look over everyone's roadsters and have a short rally or two."

Gladys clapped her hands in glee. "The Horshams of Cromwoh must be first on the list. Dickie also loves his livestock, so you can take him out to see your prize creature. And the Tintagull brothers from Open Breech each have a car. They would love to compete against one another. Perhaps Lord Rashcum can make it this time as well."

"Yes, of course. Unfortunately, we owe the Grubbs an invitation. They are, oh so, so brash and braggadocio. Let's hope they decline." He wiped his cheek on his jacket sleeve.

The Grubbs? I immediately prayed that they refuse the invitation. First, there was Thelma with her wandering hands. Second, they'd likely bring Squimm, whom I couldn't avoid in the service quarters. I had one hope. Used to being chauffeured everywhere, they might not have bought a roadster since I worked for them.

Euphoria finally spoke. "Will no women participate behind the wheel? I think it would add to the energy of the rallies."

Lord Leo smacked the table. "Nan, I daresay that is a ridiculous idea. Ladies do not drive. And did they try, they would only end up in accidents.'

"Brother, I know you read about the races. What of Dorothy Levitt and her speed record? She beat all the men in that race. Or her close rival, that Lautmann woman?"

"I doubt you will find anyone like them in Cornwall or Devon," he replied, while leaving the table.

Automobiles were the latest fad to hit our out-of-the-way corner. With so little population, and the ready availability of horse carriages, locals did not see much use in travelling by a four-wheeled put-putting machine. Autos were restricted to roads, of which there were few, often not smooth-surfaced. We knew what horses need to stay healthy, while cars required tools, parts, and a new set of knowledge.

In time, though, Cornwall gentry submitted to the idea of autos as fun and as sport. The thought of taking the wheel at fifteen miles an hour in an open vehicle especially appealed to those less athletic as a way of enjoying speed. Lord Leo had bought his first car after attending a Crystal Palace Show in London. Not wanting to get his hands greasy, he hired a local motorcyclist, Frumpkin, to ride behind him in case of trouble.

As much as I loved boats, I admired that roadster. I even volunteered to keep its yellow body shiny, its leathers soft as me Mam's hair. I hinted to Lord Leo that I would like to learn to drive, perhaps become a chauffeur, but he seemed deaf to my suggestions. Nevertheless, I befriended Frumpkin, who over time taught me the inner workings of the engine during its frequent maintenance. Me, the lad who scraped fish and polished boots, now saw himself as part of the new century, the new world of promise. One day I would own a car.

With the car event some weeks away, I settled back into my normal chores. One day, I passed by Euphoria sitting on a bench in the garden. As usual, she was dressed in a gown of rainbow colors, silky stripes adding to her height. In her lap was a sketch book, and she was staring out over the lawn. My footfalls startled her briefly. Then she smiled and beckoned with her long index finger

"Kenal, come and join me." She patted on the spot beside her. "And please call me Nan, which I prefer. I am sorry have had no chance to learn more about you. I hear you are from the south."

"Yes, milady. Mousehole, not far from Penzance and Saint Michael's Mount. A fishing family."

"Such a lovely spot, the Mount. I used to go to parties there when I was quite young. The St Aubyns, you know. The Barons of St Levans. Strange people. Who wouldn't be, spending part of the year on a tidal island?"

"I have only seen it from the shore, when visiting family in Penzance. I did go on the causeway once with a cousin. We searched for treasures. I cut myself on a razor-like rock that my teacher later said was a Stone Age man's flint."

Nan laughed. "Forgive me. Of course you couldn't know the St Aubyns. All to your good, I must say. Now turn your face toward that tall tree in the distance. I'd like to sketch you."

She took my head in her hands and gently guided it where she wanted.

"Good. Now just sit quietly while I draw and talk."

I rather liked this chance to sit with me face in the sun. Though keeping my head still, I could move my eyes to explore the birds flitting in the tree. Chippy was getting to me, interested in feathered friends!

"Norton tells me you are a good assistant to him in the library. It is unusual for our service people to read and write as well as you do. Are you studying our estate history?"

"No. He has me working more with the bound books. He seems protective of the archives, though they also need some order. It seems years since anyone has looked at all those dusty boxes with their ancient papers. My first job, though, was to organize two boxes of your letters."

"Oh, my. I hope you weren't shocked. I was rather naughty in my early years."

"To be honest, ma'am, I could not read your handwriting, did I want to. Mr Norton wanted me just to put things in order by date, not study the bits."

"That only improves his standing in my mind. When I am dead, the letters may interest some historian, though I doubt it."

"Has he said anything about the Curse? Stop! You're slumping." She tapped my chin upward.

"It be truth, I discussed the Curse with him recently. He said it was a myth. He didn't believe in it. He suggested no written proof existed. Yet I seem to recall hearing it being quoted somewhere. By Mr Snerd, I think."

"Yes, some writer published a version after Albert died. It was printed in the *Bude Bulletin*. Lord Sinjin bought up the printer and destroyed remaining copies. The *Bulletin* never appeared again. Snerd is old time Cornwall, loves to tell tales. He is almost an actor the way he delivers them."

While she spoke, I became distracted by two rooks nearby. They stood on a branch and performed some kind of ritual, bobbing up and down in opposition. One up, one down.

"Are you listening, Kenal? I hope you don't believe in that fairy tale! All it does is stir people up."

"So you agree with Mr Norton. I canna agree in full. There is much we take on faith. My life would be dark days without Scripture. Do you not agree?"

"Ah, yes, faith. That is very interesting, Kenal. I do have faith in Art and Beauty. I sometimes find pleasure in the church mysteries on Sunday. You argue well, but I still hold to the Curse being fantasy."

She tore a sheet off her pad and handed me the sketch. My own portrait! She had even included the dancing rooks in the distance.

Standing up to leave, she announced, "I am off to the Baden spas tomorrow. While I am gone, I have some requests. One is to assist Letty when you can. Out of the saddle, she is clumsy and accident-prone. Young Algie gets all the attention and praise despite being a rather stupid boy. She is, you must admit, not of lovely face. Marriage will not come quickly. That, at least, is far in the future."

"I am happy to keep an alert eye over her, milady. She is kindly and deserves care."

"Good. My second is that you write to me if anything unusual happens. Keep me informed. Can you do that? I would be most grateful. I will leave my address with Mrs Quirk in case you need it."

"I hope any news is good news, milady. May your travels go smooth."

"Thank you. Now go and leave me to more sketching down at the cove. And please call me Nan!"

I left without a word. Now I were even more confused. What were real? Must I be able to hold something in my hand, see or hear it, to believe it? Was the Curse real if only in the stories passed among the locals? Or was it real only if a slip of paper with Nun's warning be discovered? Truth was becoming ever more confusing.

A Confusing Word

Several days later I were enjoying a fine meal with the other servants. Snerd had slaughtered a lamb, so there were plenty left for us once Mrs Viscous cut off the chops for the family. She made pies of lamb mince, potatoes, and leeks. Thanks to her delicious gift, we stayed long at the table, some enjoying the berry brandy Bunston contributed. (One reason he were often half-seas over was his hobby of creating cordial drinks.) Leo and Gladys left in the roadster to overnight in Pyworthy, so we needn't rush out for evening duties.

I didna drink Mr Bunston's special. Instead, I sipped a flowery tea and listened to the others' chatter.

Tabitha, the laundress, was talking about the King. "I wonder if he'll ever come to Slanderley. He is always about, here and there, visiting fancy homes. Why don't he come here? Is he anti-Cornish?"

"I doubt it," replied Mrs Viscous. "He may not know we exist. Our Lord and Lady are not of the social folderol, you know. I hate to tattle, but oh those visits! When the Queen is not present, the King is not alone in his bed."

"Our monarch is not faithful?" I sputtered. "Is he not the head of the official church? Should he not be pure of mind? And dare we even gossip? Tis not good talk."

Snerd poked in, "You should read the papers in the Library, Kenal. The King is a man of great appetites. He is great in size, great in smoking cigars, and great in lust. He don't care what the people think. If he sees a famous actress or Earl's wife, he finds a way to seek his pleasure with her. It is all in the newspapers. We aren't making this up."

"And the public accept this?"

"He is such a relief after years of his mother's dark and deathly mourning. He has brought light and joy back into our lives," explained Mrs Viscous. "You were born too late to know how she cast her gloom over the country. She hid away and grew fat as a Rolly Polly. Oh, what a loss, that once frail and lovely queen turned into a walrus."

To my surprise, Turgid spoke up. "That is not all. I say the King is a good ruler. He settled our complaints with the nasty Frogs across the Channel. He has built a stronger Navy so we are a stronger nation today. Don't you agree, Sloth?"

"Eh? If you say."

"So you would like to meet him," I said to no one in particular'

"Not me," said Alice. "I agree with you, Kenal. I do not like this kind of talk, nor would I want the King and his sinful ways at Slanderley."

"Anytime you want, Kenal, I can show you some clippings. I like to save talk of Royal doings," said Mrs Quirk. "It would do you good to get your head out of old books and learn about what goes on today. Your Mam reared you well for work, but not for the facts of life."

I blushed in response. "Aye, I will take a look. If you can gather some reading together, I will see what I miss."

For once, I felt disapproval from my friends. I were very confused and leaned back in my chair, silent. The talk changed to discovery of two bloated bodies floating close to Hartland Quay. It were too upsetting to me, so I stood to leave.

Noticing me, Alice also stood up and excused herself. She nodded her head to follow.

"Kenal, I am sorry the others were unkind. They do it to help you, can you see that? I offer this kindly, as an older sister or aunt would advise."

Alice's comment surprised me. I looked up to her and welcomed her unexpected offer. So I replied in kind. "I admit to be aggrieved. They are right, though. I had a favored youth before me dad and brothers died. We didna talk of the Royals or the politicians. So long as the land were at peace, we enjoyed our Mousehole ways."

"Agreeing to read the papers will lead you to a larger truth."

"I must politely demur. My larger truth is in the Bible. . Say, Tis a full moon tonight. Would you like to join me on the cliff to watch it float over the water?"

"Thank you, Kenal, I welcome your company. I know times are changing, yet I believe some old ways should remain. It was so at my previous manor. Husbands and wives trading with one another at night for cushy-wooshy. The next morning, they all sit around the breakfast table as though nothing unusual had happened. I came here even though it is hidden away and does not pay so well."

She spoke as we walked to the stone bench overlooking the bay below. Her hair glimmered in the moonlight while her eyes grew almost black.

"That is where you and I agree. Chapel keeps us straight on the Path of Truth. I will miss your company dearly were you to leave, Alice."

"I have changed my mind about taking the other position, Kenal. After Mugwatch died, I found comfort from the visiting blacksmith. He shares my religious beliefs, though living in Mothcannon, he lives too far to attend our Chapel. He hopes to come over some Sunday soon and go walking with me afterward. I should like you to meet him."

"You deserve a good man and family, Alice, and freedom from service. I wish you well."

"It is too early to tell, of course. We have spoken only briefly, when I take him tea to the iron shed. And what of you, Kenal?

"I am too young to think of such plans. As it is, I send money to my Mam in Mousehole. I would like to return there one day, but the fishing has gone bad there and I would only burden my brothers. I save my pennies to prepare for new possibilities. It is a new century, with much hope in the air."

"I could see you as a teacher, Kenal, had you more schooling. Perhaps Mr Norton could advise you. While marriage might free me of service, you face a more difficult path if you wish to break away." She stood up and wrapped her shawl tightly. "Sorry, I must leave now before the others mistake our meeting as more than friendship. You know how they gossip."

"God be with you. I give thanks for your honesty. I wish you well with your blacksmith too."

I remained seated and considered what we had not discussed. She did not mention botherings, how maids are mishandled in r manors. I did not share my worries that the Grubbs would accept an invitation to the auto party. We did not discuss recent curious events and the Curse. I kept silent my encounter with Lady Gladys.

Alice and I shared the truth of Christ, but not the truth of actual life.

A few days later Mrs Quirk asked me to go over plans for the servants accompanying the auto party visit.

"We need to arrange many rooms. Turgid will hire men from Slyme Gurney to clean and refurbish the service bedrooms that have been unoccupied for years. There may be a half dozen each or so of valets and maids. We have space for everyone."

"Do you know when we'll have the full list?" I was thinking of Squimm's possible appearance.

"Next Wednesday is the final response day, so we'll know then. I want your assistance in assigning the men's rooms, while Alice will oversee the women's."

"I expect you'll want us in formal livery when proper."

"Yes. In fact, you remind me that a decision has been made in your regard. You will now formally be head footman, and have a room of your own. No more sharing. You'll have a room on this floor, next to Bunston. Once Turgid's men have arranged it, I'll let you know. So get to the uniform closet and fit yourself out with the fancier dress."

"Then Scullion will be alone as well?"

"No, we are getting a new boy who will move into your old space."

I know you are wondering, who is this Scullion? He arrived to replace Mugwatch. A potato-faced lad, he was jolly and full of starch—the kind you can never have enough of. Because he could read, he was full of interesting chatter. When he saw me bring out the Bible at night, he suggested we read aloud to one another. He had a small collection of poetry books and Shakespeare. Unlike Mugwatch, he was of Chapel and clean of mind.

This news were a surprise. I must assure Scullion that our friendship would not weaken as a result of my move. His natural happiness softened my more dour way. Though Chapel denies what some think of as fun, it does not require a dark and clouded being. I looked to him as a reminder to be joyful in the Light of Christ.

Despite my best efforts, I continued to chew my cheek over the appearance of the Grubbs with the gruesome Squimm. I wished Mam were here so I could seek her counsel. Lacking that, I sought out Chippy. While we were packing up the day's work, I took my chance.

"Ahem, I am sorely troubled and need the advice of an older man. I wondered whether you would be willing to listen to me and give me some guidance."

My speech clearly pleased him.

"I gather it is of a very personal nature."

"Yes, and not one I would share with Alice, my closest friend on staff."

"How about you come to the cottage with me. We will have much more privacy there and no one will interrupt. Carry these books so others will think you are still doing me service."

He pulled some books off a shelf without looking and loaded them in my arms. I followed behind him, sheepish and humble. We took a side path off the main drive through the woods. I could hear the creek burbling and burping nearby.

He paused on a stone bridge. "Isn't this charming? If you come here again, be careful crossing over. The side walls are too short, so if you tripped you would go over onto the rocks."

He pointed below. I felt dizzy peering over at the roughly pointed rocks. I reimagined Mugwatch transported there, his eyes of rigid glass.

"Fortunately, the bridge lost its use once the manor expanded and the main drive improved. The path over is fine for walkers, but I wouldn't send an auto onto it."

Approaching the cottage, I could see some stone work was from much earlier, with changes in the mortar showing its size had doubled much later.

"This is an ideal abode," Chippy continued. "I have complete privacy and comfort. The walls are so thick that a small log fire heats the entire space, and the modern plumbing satisfies as well. Then there are the birds busy outside the large windows, where I leave seed. I never tire of a common Robin. So sweet. Tweet tweet."

He lit the fire, already laid, and gestured me to sit.

"Now what exactly is your problem?"

"It's the auto party. I fear the arrival of the Grubbs with their servant Squimm. It is difficult for me to explain. I am a simple lad."

"I see you redden. Do not hesitate. I will not judge you."

"When I served at Pennididdle, the mistress would call me to her room on made-up problems. She did not behave properly as a lady ought. I canna say more."

He lit a cigarette. I refused his offer.

"I see. She was what some call *forward* toward you. Too familiar."

"Yes, so I was not sorry to leave there."

"She will of course be in the guest wing with her husband. If she is that sort of female, then I agree you do not have to worry. There will be many other men she can tempt, ones who may not find her familiarity unwelcome. It is how they behave at these events," Chippy clarified.

"So I have heard. Yet there remains their servant, Squimm. He were also cruel to me. He stole me mother's broach, the one she gave me on departing. He were also familiar in unmanly ways."

"Kenal, you are so damned innocent that it is rather delightful – though I regret the effects of these two people upon you. I do have more experience in terms of Squimm's behavior. It is common in public schools, such as the one I attended. Older boys are rough and nasty with younger ones, sometimes in most unseemly ways. It is part of the culture, of toughening the boys up into men."

"But Squimm did not go to a public school. And one can become a man without cruelty."

"True, but it is how some boys like to do things. It is not always considered wrong."

"I donna understand such beliefs. How do I handle Squimm, if he shows up? He will be dining with us in service. My bedroom is on the main service floor."

"He will be busy attending his couple during the day, so he won't be around you all the time. My first suggestion is that you cut him cold when you first see him. You are top footman now, correct? Stick your chin up and act superior. Do not give away any fear however much you shake inside."

"I had not thought of that. Also, I am full-grown now, which may deter him."

"Use your position to sit next to Bunston at table. As a visiting servant, Squimm will have to be much further down. Do not give him the slightest glance."

"I will try your approach. I were ill-prepared when I met him several years ago."

"It is a matter of appearance, Kenal. In public school I was not the highest titled, yet I acted such. I escaped some of the worst treatment as a result."

"It is what Mr Creakle taught us about public schools like yours, how our great leaders come from them. In Mousehole most of us were the same, plain fishing folk. Only a few people were of middling comfort. We had no lords or earls or such. He tried to explain we would face the pain of social class did we to go to a city or work on an estate. I am beginning to understand."

"So, did Squimm bugger you?"

I didn't want to admit my ignorance, so I said, "No, he did not. Don't tell me—"

"Yes, at public schools. Buggery this, buggery that."

If you don't believe in my innocence, recall how I were attached to my Mam and raised in a strict religious family. The next chance I had, I went to the dictionary to look up "bugger." I knew it were something dirty, but understood no more when it failed to turn up in the book.

Lacking an answer, I went into the stable area and found Gleeves polishing a saddle.

"Hey, Kenal, how be ye?"

"All is well, for the most part."

"I hear you have moved up to top footman. I'm not surprised."

"Thank you. How is Scullion doing in my place?"

"He is also a bright one, not to mention his good spirits. When he joins me on trips to Bude, he has me laughing so hard I almost lose the reins."

"He has added a lot at supper, too, with his wit."

"Can I do anything for ye?"

"Perhaps you can. Mr Norton mentioned a word to me, and I have not been able to find out what it means. I think it concerns something nasty, because he said the boys did it at public school."

"Try me."

"It is *buggery*. I wondered if it had to do with putting spiders or wasps down someone's back, but I could not find a meaning for the word."

"Tis far from what you guessed, Kenal. It concerns bodily invasion of one man upon another. It is against the law. You may know the word from your Bible as sodomy."

"I was never clear on that either. So it is a sin, yet the fancy boys at public schools do it anyway."

"Aye, it seems strange. It is the way of the titled. They go to those schools, so they must indulge in buggery."

"Yet they don't get arrested?"

"Not at all. Even those who continue as adults seem to avoid the court. It is the way of the ruling class."

"I give thanks to have been saved that fate. The more time I spend on these estates, the less appealing it seems to be in that status. I pity little Algernon."

"He may just face beatings and such."

"I hope so. Chippy told me how he was able to avoid the worst of that nastiness. Well, thank ye for your help. I am off to serve a late dinner and must needs change."

Truth is, I was still uncertain about just how the bodily contacts between the boys took place. Then I recalled Squimm coming behind me and poking his privies into my behind. So that is buggery, sodomy? God save me from such sin.

The Slanderley Curse

Horseless Carriages

The big weekend was almost here. We in service fretted because the event was a first for Slanderley. We knew how to prepare for hunt days or a fete, but exactly how did we manage automobiles and drivers?

Gleeves now became responsible for Lord Leo's roadster. Despite Frumpkin's training, he could not adjust to the machine. He complained about keeping cans of petrol, worried they might inflame. He cursed over keeping the body and tires spotless. (It was understood horse conveyances could not avoid road splatter and more.) He worried about a breakdown he could not fix, and mumbled about the confusion of the engine. I wondered how much longer he would stay with us. Given my study under Frumpkin, I could have stepped in, but Gleeves had superiority.

Lady Gladys turned out to be a most surprising help. One of her American friends was Willie Vanderbilt Jr, an early adopter of the horseless carriage. Loving speed, he created road races in the New York countryside and won some in his Mercedes. Writing him for advice, Gladys realized our narrow hedged roads were problematic. She and Mr Bunston spent hours reviewing maps to lay out possible routes and activities. They decided upon daylong events with lunch stops for the casual drivers, along with one circling the peninsula for three days, including two overnights at prearranged lodgings. Given the top legal speed of twenty miles per hour, this plan seemed most practical.

When I learned of these final arrangements, I relaxed. There would be an opening formal dinner and one at the end, but otherwise the numbers present for luncheon or tea would be small. I forgot how busy Mrs Viscous would be, both for the formal meals and the luncheon baskets delivered by Gleeves in his carriage. As usual, day helpers came from Slyme Gurney. Mrs Quirk rose to her military-style command of the schedule.

We should have not been surprised when the acceptance replies for couples included "regrets" for the wives in several cases. Women did not drive, and many would not want to sit and wait for the cars to go and return. To our relief, Fanny Wurzel was not joining the Bishop. Alas, Thelma did accept with Harry Grubb, which meant Squimm arriving as well.

We were surprised to have several single ladies respond in the affirmative. Bunston explained they were special friends of Lady Gladys, who invited them especially for alternative activities in the Summer House. This imbalance of unaccompanied men and women forced me to redo the room assignments. In the end, I placed all the solitary women in the West Wing in rooms behind the de Loverly suites, married couples in East Wing suites, and the solitary men in available single rooms behind.

Young Algernon asked to move down from the nursery floor, just for the weekend, so he could be close to all the participants. He had taken to coming to the library to look into the latest books on the growing British car industry. I was pleased to see him take an interest in reading of any topic, and encouraged his return, even though he mainly looked at pictures.

"Look at this one, Kenal. It can go thirty miles an hour! Whoosh, I wish I could go thirty miles an hour. I'd head into the fields and chase the cows. What fun that would be."

"I'm sure the cows would not like it, milord."

"Well I wouldn't go after a bull. Now that would be dangerous. They could damage the car."

"True, though it will be many a year before you can sit behind the wheel."

"By then I bet the cars will go eighty miles an hour. Zoom, zoom, zoom! I will shred the hedgerows. I will be the fastest driver in all of Cornwall. Even Devon. Here comes Lord Algernon, the fastest man in England."

"Perhaps your father will take you to a professional race one day. They are starting to build racing tracks, you know. You could visit him in the trophy room and tell him about your reading."

I knew Algernon could benefit from more contact with his father, and hoped my encouragement might stir a flame between them.

On the other hand, young Letty thought the auto event plans were boring. I knew she would be better off away and on a horse. Recalling my promise to the absent Euphoria, I spoke to Jemima about her. She notified the Horshams, who offered to host Letty during the event. Although they owned the nearest estate, they had declined the invitation. Lord Horsham would see the new bull another time. No gas machine was welcome on their horse-favored fields. The bit of chicanery worked. Letty went off with a suitcase, her Cob led along by the coach.

My other little manipulation worked as well. Lord Leo was not only pleased to learn of Algie's interest in cars, he decided they would share a room during the event in the East Wing, amongst the other men. This union sealed what was to become a lifelong fascination with speed for the boy.

In time, I thought of a solution to keep Squimm out of my way, and brought it up backways with Mrs Quirk.

"We have so many more servants arriving than we have lodging in the servant wing. I need your help in making the placements."

"I've thought about that too, Kenal. And there will be more man servants, which causes problems for the maids. We could triple up by adding cots, but I don't like the idea."

"I agree. Is there somewhere else we can send visiting men? I thought of some outbuildings, like the beach cottage, but they would be too far from their masters. I just don't know what to do."

"There's one space, the nursery floor. The children won't be there, so we can put more cots in the extra rooms up there."

"What a good idea! I'll go up with Scullion and see how we can fit the arriving valets. I know several rooms have little within, and others can have the storage pushed aside. Thank ye, Mrs Quirk, for your wise idea."

My wise idea, slithered through our conversation.

I could breathe free.

Twas a cool and breezy morn when the first roadsters appeared, cases strapped to their backs. The entrance circle was wide enough to park the machines nose to butt. Some carriages arrived as well, bringing servants and extra luggage. Mr Bunston greeted the guests and sent them to the main saloon, from which I would take them to their rooms. Scullion took charge of servants arriving in the back, so I did not have to encounter Squimm.

The noise of so many voices down the halls and up the stairs was uncanny. I forgot how used we were to silence at Slanderley. Three couples and six unaccompanied men, along with twelve servants, cluttered the hall

While musing in a hallway, I felt a hard punch on my left kidney. Without turning, I knew it was Squimm, just down from the nursery floor to visit the rooms assigned to the Grubbs.

"Still working, Fishface? They must be hard up here to find help."

"Greetings, Squimm. I trust your room satisfies," I said, peering down my nose.

His whelk ears reddened. "The kiddy floor, you mean? I was given shares in a small room and shifted my cot into the large schoolroom where I am alone. So, yes, I satisfy, by myself."

"Were you told about meals? Man servants are eating separately in the butlers' pantry. I am sure you will find that room arranged most comfortable and Mrs Viscous's food most agreeable."

With that, I turned quickly and marched down the stairs with a masklike demeanor borrowed from Mr Bunston. I knew Squimm would be angry to be kept away from the maids while eating, though

I didn't doubt he would find means to encounter them elsewhere. I made a note to alert Alice and have her spread the word for the girls to be watchful of him.

While we prepared for cocktails, Mr Bunston introduced me to a young man sent over from the Horsham's Cromwoh manor to help serve the evening formal meal. Dom was slender, with coal dark hair and wiggly brown eyes. He was also very cute and would soon have the maids tittering for his attention. I welcomed him and discovered he was very experienced, a most able hand for an under-staffed table.

Mr Bunston served heavily jiggered cocktails that evening, so the guests floated in, unaware of Lady Gladys's speed dining routine. No sooner was the fourteenth person served than Bunston shoved us to start collecting the plates. We ran a marathon around the table while managing not to spill a drop of consommé or gravy. Even the American Grubbs were befuddled, and had little time to bray a remark.

Afterwards, I invited Dom to sup beside me before he went back to Cromwoh to sleep. The scullery maid was quick to sit on the other side and grin her protruding teeth at him. Unperturbed, he were kindly to her, and sent her in giggles.

Mrs Quirk rapped her glass. "Look at Dom and Kenal everyone. Could they not be brothers? They are almost twins."

We looked at one another and recognized the almost-mirrored feature. We laughed over the recognition.

"We must be distant cousins," he said. "Where are you from?"

"Mousehole. Me family were fisher folks."

"Mine are from Penzance."

"Where me Mam grew up. We must have a blood tie somewhere way back. Me Tas always said Mam had some Portuguese blood in her. You too?"

"Look at us, not totally Cornwall in coloring. I suspect some interesting encounters deep in our past histories."

The puzzle solved, the conversation returned to the usual gabble over rumors, complaints, and the latest drowning victims.

The next morning after breakfast, everyone gathered around the cars to *ooh* and *aah*. I were too busy carting things around with Scullion. Mrs Quirk said Lady Gladys was entertaining special women friends in the Summer House, that we must supply it with tea fixings, luncheon service, linens, shawls, comfy pillows, and more. She said we were not to go there under any circumstances, that she and Lady Gladys's maid were the only people allowed there during the ongoing event. Milady had special plans unfit for male eyes.

Late morning, all the drivers peeled off to explore the neighboring roads and test their engines before the next day's big events. They were all awash in large baggy coats, protective goggles, and tight caps. From a window I watched them take off, and was surprised to see Dom returned to sit beside Lord Rashcum, who normally declined our invitations. More unexpected, Thelma Grubb sat beside her husband. I gather she was not one of the "special ladies" for the Summer House frolics. I imagined them chattering away, perhaps over needlework, while milady showed off her latest spider collection.

Truth is, women of that class did not have much to do or entertain themselves. The men could go out shooting or to their city clubs, but the women seemed tied to bits of charity and lolling about the manor in boredom. Or so Mrs Quirk said. She wished Lady Gladys, being American, were less that sort. "How can I run the house well without her consult? She is always off somewhere in secret. At least she is a proper hostess this weekend."

The day passed smoothly. I welcomed being busier than usual. Even Mr Bunston was showing some energy rather than hugging a bottle somewhere. When Dom returned from the short jaunt, he explained how he knew Lord Rashcum as a friend of the Horshams. He'd never been in a car before, and entertained us all with accounts of almost falling out, mud asplash their clothing, and a near crash into a wall.

My plans to isolate Squimm worked wonders too. Word came that he skipped dinner. Rather, he went to Slyme Gurney to get into trouble his usual way. I slept very well from happy exhaustion and avoiding assault from the Grubb crew.

The next day I assisted the four cars taking off for the big rally. I helped pack the luggage and handle any special requests. Drivers each took a man servant to assist in case of tire collapse or need for other work. That meant Squimm was off with Harry Grubb.

The travels would take them on a circuit, with stayovers in St. Ives and Plymouth. The routes were not direct, but full of confusing, often unmarked side roads. The inn keepers at each lodge would note the time of arrivals and telegraph us with the results. The final stage would be the most treacherous, given its winding through the moorlands with their quicksand.

Lord Leo, who was not doing the circuit, puffed himself up to give the expected sendoff.

"Well, men, we wish you a safe trip with no breakdowns. We are on the cusp of a new world for England, one where we no longer deal with the discomfort of carriages and the unpredictability of horses. Although only one of you will have the shortest time, you are in my mind all winners."

Following the applause, the explosive putts of the roadsters marked their departure. The remaining drivers prepared for a short trip, which included a picnic at Tintagel. Following a drumming of shots and burps, they were off.

With most guests off in their cars or at the Summer House, I took a break in the library. I had copies of the rally route and wanted to trace it on a map. While following the lanes with my finger, I imagined the thrill of the wind rushing into my face, the surprise of sudden turns, the threat of a sheep herd lolling about in the road. Lost in thought, I startled when someone clasped their hands over my eyes.

The brassy voice was unmistakable.

"Hello, Kenal. Aren't I lucky to find you here all alone?"

I grabbed her hands and pulled them off.

"May I help you, Mrs Grubb?"

"Now you know I want you to call me Thelma. We are such good friends, are we not?"

"Ma'am, are you looking for a book to read? I know the shelves well."

She tousled my hair, then leaned over to whisper in my ear. "Why should I want a book when I have you for entertainment?"

"Please—that is not in my duty roster—"

"Oh, you smell just like Swiss cheese. I *love* Swiss cheese."

I felt her tongue on my neck. I had no choice now. I stood abruptly and shoved the chair back into her.

"Why did you do that—you fool! That chair smashed my ribs. I can hardly breathe. You will regret that. I'm off to report your rash behavior."

An interruption froze each of us in place.

"Ahem," said Mr Bunston.

How long had he been there? Did he see the wretched woman's insults toward me?

"Madam, Lady Gladys has sent over a note. She offers her apology she cannot entertain you today. She wishes to offer you access to her private den so you can write letters and read."

"Read? Write letters?" Thelma brayed a laugh that sent the doves in the trees by the window off in fright. "I saw a boat by the cove. I'm going down there to row a bit. Tell your kitchen maid to send a lunch basket down in an hour. Read, really!"

Were she not wearing slacks, she'd have swept her skirt in defiance as she pressed past me and departed.

"I hope this is between us, Mr Bunston. I didna—"

"No frets, Kenal. She asked me where you were and only later did I think she was up to no honorable behavior. At least she is out of our ears for the day."

When he left, I thought about the boat. Snerd and I had worked on it, but was it fully repaired? Was it safe? Even so, the waters beyond the cove covered a graveyard. Before I could follow these thoughts, Mrs Quirk barged in.

"What are you doing here lollygagging? We need your strong hands."

"With the guests mostly off for the day, I thought—"

"We have all the rooms to reset, tons of extra laundry. Alice is almost in tears over all the extra work. She and Jane must redo all the rooms and can use you to carry chamber pots and such. Now, get moving." She shook her keys in anger.

I bowed in apology and felt my ears redden as I passed by her to rush upstairs and find the maids. Mrs Quirk was right, they had too few hands and soon had me running all over the manor, delivering this, getting that. We didna even have time for midday meal, apart from bread and cheese I took for them to slip in their apron pockets. We cleared the rooms just as the men returned from their countryside exploration.

Now it was rush to serve a formal meal. I were too busy balancing plates to notice one person was missing until Lady Gladys spoke up.

"Where is Thelma Grubb? Has anyone seen her?"

Scullion and I caught eyes yet remained silent, as was required.

Finally Lord Leo spoke out. "I'm sure she is just resting and missed the gong. You know those Americans, very independent. Now, why are you men so late with the dessert?"

We set out the puddings, poured the wine, and shifted our tired feet. The party was unusually talkative tonight, so the meal dragged on.

Unexpectedly, Bunston rushed in, a wrinkled telegram in his hand. He handed it to Lord Leo.

"Why, it's the first results."

ARRIVAL ORDER. "EDGECRUMB, TREEFUCSIS, GRUBB, RASHCUM."

"All in safely. Good show. Shall we—"

The party decamped to the rooms separating male and female for cigars and sherry. One person broke the expected division of sexes. Lady Gladys not only enjoyed a small cheroot with the men, she was vicious at billiards.

I was about to mention Thelma and the boat to Dom, when we heard a clatter in the entrance hall. Rushing in to assist, we found Thelma chattering with the other women about her "wonderful adventure." She wore an outsized slicker over her clothes, and her hair was a viper's nest from sea water.

"When I saw the small sail boat in the cove, I decided to take advantage of the gentle breezes. It was so lovely lolling on the water in the cove. Before I knew it, I was out of its safety and in the sea. It was calmer than usual, so I kept on until I realized the hull was leaking. Of course I had no place to moor, given the treacherous cliffs.

"I thought I should die. It was so thrilling. I stuffed my scarf into the leak, and kept on, though of course the save was temporary. But I kept on and took off my shirt, it was red, you know, and tied it to the mast as a signal. And wouldn't you know, soon a fishing boat came upon me and the sweetest man pulled me aboard. I had the most delightful afternoon, though your boat sank, Lord Leo, I'm sorry to say, but what an adventure it gave me."

I thought about the sweet man and Thelma in her wet undershirt and her actual preference for adventure.

"He had to finish his haul, of course, so I helped pull in the nets. When we moored, he gave me this slicker and dropped me at the pub to warm up and dine while he took care of his catch. Then a constable came in for a pint and I told him my story and he offered to bring me back here. I had to double on his bicycle, and the tires went flat, and we ended up in a ditch. He was very sweet about it."

Another sweetie. Had she no limits?

"Then one of your tenants passed by with a hay wagon and brought me here. I have had the most wonderful day!"

At least the Samaritan tenant was not sweet and saved hisself a lot of trouble.

To think it were Squimm who had so taunted me brain aforehand.

The Slanderley Curse

A Terrible Turn

The following day went smoothly for both the local and the three-day rally drivers. We in service, however, struggled with all the extra chores. Day workers shirk when they can because it is easy to evade the oversight of Mr Bunston or Mrs Quirk. At least Dom was proving a help, and I hoped one day to pay the return during a big event at Cromwoh.

On the final day of the rally, excitement built to see the four competitors arrive and calculate the winner from the three days of postings. Lord Leo suggested the other men relax around the estate so everyone would be present when the first car arrived. Bunston would bang the gong in the entrance hall to announce the returns.

I were busy lugging a basket of linen when I heard the gong beat a long tattoo. After dropping the basket in the laundry shed, I ran out around the manor to see who was in. There were a crowd of males at the entrance steps, along with Thelma Grubb and a few man servants. Lord Leo was holding a paper in his hand, a telegram, and gave an ashen face to the group.

"I have news. As it will be some time before the cars arrive, I recommend we gather in the main saloon. Bunston and Kenal, please see to the drinks counter. They will be needed."

That message, hinting at trouble, spread murmurs as all went inside. In the main saloon, I took orders while Bunston mixed the cocktails. Lunch had not been served, so we ordered down for a cheese and fruit spread from the kitchen. Lord Leo remained rigid and stone-faced until all were seated and attended to. Upon his nod, Bunston clapped for attention.

"I have most regrettable news. Early this morning, after leaving Plymouth, one car had a dreadful accident."

He looked over where Thelma was sitting beside Gudgie Longstretch, her latest fish. He moved closer towards her while he continued.

"Thelma, my dear—"

"Not Squimm!"

"No, Harry. Killed instantly. Squimm seriously injured. That is all I have for now."

Thelma collapsed on Gudgie, who called for a glass of brandy to calm her down.

The shock led to further drinking and little eating. Because Lord Leo remained silent, no one knew what to do. Eventually, Bishop Wurzel took the reins.

"I suggest we pack up and prepare to leave early. Those who wish to help Thelma can wait until the other drivers or the authorities arrive to fill in the details."

"That makes good sense, Bishop," agreed his lordship. "I'll see that the wives in the summer house receive the news as well so they can also prepare accordingly."

I can't say people rushed out, but it was not long before the only guests left in the room were Thelma and Gudgie, he looking none too happy while she sniveled upon his shoulder.

I emptied the bar and returned to my other duties.

There being no lunch now for the guests, we in service had the planned menu, a tasty spread of cold meats and cakes. Mr Bunston recounted the facts of the accident, while I kept from sharing my evil thoughts of Thelma's fears for Squimm. A mind may think ill, but the voice must stay mute. A sudden and unexpected death during a Slanderley event did not bode well for the estate reputation. "The Curse," someone whispered. Yet with everyone leaving, we faced fewer days of extra work ahead.

Afterwards, I heard each of the three remaining roadsters drive into the entrance circle, but could not leave my post, however curious I be. I also heard other cars depart. I expect much talking passed about the accident, but I heard nawt until late that afternoon.

Mr Bunston alerted me that two constables had arrived. He asked me to accompany him to the saloon once again, where a full account was to be made. There sat my Lord and Lady, along with Thelma, *sans* Gudgie.

"Sergeant Pepper from Princetown, milords and ladies. I regret to provide details of the accident and answer any questions. Constable Mustard was first on the scene, so I shall ask him to start."

The Constable took out his notebook so he could speak without addressing anyone directly.

"At approximately 8:36 this morning a cyclist encountered me on my rounds in Princetown to alert me of an automobile accident in the moor nearby. After notifying my Sergeant, I followed the rider a short distance toward Devil's Bridge. There I saw a lobster red roadster smashed into a boulder. The driver rested atop the rock, and was not moving. The passenger was off to the left on the ground and groaning. I could see he had broken bones and could not help him. I climbed upon the boulder to look more closely at the driver. His open eyes were glazed and he did not seem to be breathing. A check of his pulse proved he had transpired. At approximately 9:17 Sergeant Pepper arrived with a medical van. To you, sir."

"The medics quickly saw to the passenger. They affirmed he needed immediate hospital care for broken bones and took him off. We ascertained from his personal belongings that he was one Mr Squimm of Pennididdle. Similarly, we learned the deceased was Mr Harry Grubb of the same manor. The medics took Mr Squimm to the hospital, and returned to take the deceased to the Princetown funeral chapel."

"Do you know what caused the crash?" asked Lady Gladys.

"From marks in the road, it looks as though they missed the curve while descending the steep road. They must have been at high speed when they hit the boulder. With nothing to protect them, they were thrown out on impact. I fear it is an omen of more to come with these gas buggies."

Milady put her hand on Thelma's arm. "You poor child. What can we do to help? We are at your service."

Thelma pushed the hand away. "When can I see him? I must see him."

Milord replied, "I expect the chapel will contact you. I suggest you return home immediately so you can make arrangements. You will need to make arrangements with a local chapel."

"No, not Harry. Squimm. I must go to Princetown to see Squimm!"

"Since you are now without a car, I will take you there and anywhere else afterward. I'll see that Gleeves returns your belongings to Pennididdle."

"Oh, thank you, Leo. I hope this is no trouble."

"None at all."

Another fish, I imagined.

When everyone left the room, I cleaned up and almost wished I could have a drink. The clear gin sparkling in its bottle tempted me, but I had a piece of stinky cheese instead.

The guests departed, I'd more extra work: checking the rooms with the maids, locating items left behind to pack up and post, note any damage for repairs, and such. Mrs Quirk said we could do the massive linen laundry the next day. I had a glimmer of other pleasures when I found the scarf of one man's wife in the room of a solitary male guest. So the King's ways reached all the way to this tiny bit of Cornwall. I tossed the vile scarf into a hearth and set it afire.

I was about to go down the main staircase when I saw Lady Gladys at the end of the hall. She waved me over to her.

"Kenal, I do not expect my husband to return tonight or even several nights. I expect he will see Thelma back to her manor and assist with all the arrangements. What a sorry mess?"

"Yes, ma'am. A terrible loss."

She peered at me strangely. "I don't mean Harry's death. I refer to my plans with the other women. We were just starting the highlight of our rituals. Oh, you don't know about that, of course. Anyway, I wish to remain in my rooms until my husband returns, all meals and posts delivered there by Alice."

"I shall inform Mrs Quirk when I go downstairs. Is there anything else?"

"Yes, watch out for Letitia's return, and explain to her what happened. I trust you can do so without upsetting her. No mention of the Curse."

"Of course, milady. I shall be very gentle."

She sighed deeply. "If we are fortunate, we shall have a full week of quiet." She turned to return to her private suite. In the process something fell from her pocket. I knelt to pick it up, a rosary made of ruby beads.

Handing it to her, I watched her blush.

"Oh, you see my secret. I admit we ladies sometimes gather to say the prayers on the beads, even a litany now and then. I do miss Latin mass. Now you and I share this secret. I know you to be discrete."

I bowed without a word and watched her leave. I wondered who the real Gladys was. She behaved in such unexpected ways. At least now I realized her relationship with Lord Leo in public was likely an act. She be more serious than any others realized. Still, Latin mass?

The week passed. Can you believe? Lord Leo tripped on the tennis courts at Pennididdle and was laid up there with badly injured knee and ankle. He was not to return until he recovered. His telegram assured he was "in top hands."

When Letty returned, she was the only one at the evening table. While I served, she enthused about the Horsham steeds. "And the manor is cozy, none of the precious fake gold furniture like you find here. When I grow up, I will want the same comfort, cushy cushions and cushy pillows. Our rooms here are much too large and chilly."

While she prattled on, I stood firm, my eyes straight ahead. This eventually upset her.

"Kenal, there are two of us in the room. Just because you are a footman does not mean you are not human. Didn't my aunt ask you to watch over me?"

"Service has rules, milady. We may share the same house, but we could as be in different towns."

"Pish, pish. I can order you to break a rule. I order you to speak with me when we are alone. There. Now you can do so."

"As you wish, milady. Have you something to share?"

"Lady Horsham said I was like the daughter she never had. There is only her son Reginald, who is at university. She said I must return sometime when I can meet him."

"I am pleased you enjoyed yourself."

"I made the footman there speak up as well. He reminded me of you."

"Dom, you mean. He was a great help during the auto events."

"He knows all about ponies. He is in service, but his father was a stable hand, so he loves horses. He even combed my pony when we returned from our rides. Now, what can you tell me?"

"I have a question. Do you still believe people here are full of secrets?"

"Oh, even more. One day I shall show you one. I am the only person who knows."

What a remarkable child, full of care for others not of her level. She were a future rebel, I were sure.

A Mysterious Guest

The days rolled on with no sign of his lordship. One day I received a note written on manor stationery.

Dear Mr Gundry

Given we do not need full staff at this moment, I grant you leave for a quick visit of five days to your family.

Gladys de Loverly

Such a surprise! I packed a small bag and counted my savings. Going and coming would each take a full day, even adding a train part of the way, so I had few hours to see them.

Tis not worth going into detail on the visit. When I arrived at my sister's house in Mousehole, me Mam was happily surrounded by her grandchildren. She were glad to see me, of course, but twas clear she had new babes to dote upon. As for my two fishing brothers, they no longer went out to sea. Following three years of poor catches, Conan moved to Penzance, where he was learning the building trade. Goron still lives in the old cottage, out of which he expanded the garden. He also hunts rabbits to sell both meat and vegetables at markets and to restaurants. Each brother refused to give up and enter poverty, as some fishermen had done.

It were clear there be no place for me back among my family. They kept on about how lucky I were to have a good master and easy service. Mam was most concerned that I continued my Bible reading and Chapel attendance. Twas nice to sing again with the men, and enjoy the homemade food I knew growing up—albeit less fish.

I returned to learn Lord Leo also came back the same day. From what I heard, he were still hobbling on crutches but admitted life at Pennididdle did not suit. "Too loud and busy," he were said to say. He remained only to see Harry properly placed in the ground and guide Thelma into widowhood, a duty he believed his due, given his role in the accident.

It were unclear whether Thelma could remain in the manor. The lawyers were busy reenacting *Bleak House*, that novel of endless court delays, so she might be there for years while they fussed and sucked up the estate. Rumor was she moved Squimm into Harry's old quarters. Who would be the fish now, who the prey? We in service had much tittle during meal time as we imagined the possibilities. I know it were not kind to talk such ways, but the sin were minor.

Soon after, Alice had permission to visit her family. When she returned, she said her suitor, Mr Tiddlysquat, came for tea and asked for her hand. Her parents approved, and she expected to leave

Slanderley once he earned enough to buy them a cottage. Her pink cheeks grew rosy as she spoke. I should miss her, but I knew it could be several years before the blacksmith reached their goal. Would he ever, now that gas monsters were sure to take over?

Apart from Letty's cheeriness, the mood in the manor was glum. Until he healed, Lord Leo slept on a daybed in his den, surrounded by his ancestors' moldy trophies. Their dead eyes seemed to foster a black demeanor. He shouted so often at his beloved Pudelpointer that one day the beast refused to enter the room and moved into Sloth's cottage.

I took the dog out on long walks late in the day when my main work were done. We usually circuited the lake so Gwandror could jump in and enjoy the water along the way. I also did Snerd a favor by checking the doors to the follies were locked. Although it be unlikely, an unwanted guest must be discovered. So it were a surprise one day to find the mill house door free. I sent the dog in ahead of me to alert me of a possible presence. I could hear him sniffling around and concluded the place were clear.

Inside, I discovered the space had one large room. Cobwebs flowed down from the ceiling, yet the dusty floor revealed no clear boot marks, just scufflings. Whoever got in made a quick wander and left. There were nothing of value to take, just rusty metal bits and a buggy woodpile. The intruder had jimmied the lock, which must be replaced with a stronger one. I informed Snerd of such after dinner.

"Perhaps it were a pilgrim looking for a bed," he guessed. "Though he'd have to be far off the usual path to end up there. Thank ye for telling me. We don't want any more bodies showing up there."

Weeks later, Euphoria returned from her trip to Paris and Baden. When she left the car, a pudgy, short, and balding man followed behind. She marched on inside, and seemed to ignore him. I later heard his name was Csaba Szarka, that he was also a painter. (He wrote his name down for me one day, as it sounds more like Chaba Zarka.) They had met in Baden. I wondered how he was able to pressure Euphoria into joining her return to Slanderley. She did not suffer fools, so he must have some good qualities.

The next day, while doing my lake circuit walk, I came upon him working at an easel. He wore a painter's cloak and floppy hat, both splotched with color. I was going to pass quietly, when he called out. I walked over featureless.

"Lovely spot, no? When Euffie described the estate, I begged to come to do some landscape painting. See?"

His attempt at copying nature was a mess of slashing, strange boxes, and very unnatural colors.

"Hmm," I noted.

"The style is *en vogue* in France. I take it further, creating impressions with cubes and a limited palette. Step back, and see."

"Ah," I observed. "May I get you anything?" I didn't want to be drawn into a conversation with someone so, as the French say, *de trop*—my latest vocabulary addition. He was not one of us.

"I am bilious, thank you. Too much sauerkraut in my life. That calls for a sparkly drink. Champagne? And if you see Euffie, tell her where I am. I haven't seen her today and worry she is not feeling well."

Without a word, I left straight for the manor. I found his Euffie in the morning room where she was writing notes. I told her of my encounter and Mr Szarka's request.

"Oh, that man! I can't resist any Central European charm, and he overwhelms with it. When he first met me in Baden, he toasted in Magyar, so I knew at once he was Hungarian."

"And you trusted him?"

"Not at first. Over time I realized he was rather lonely and adrift and feeling sorry for himself. My rare maternal impulse just wanted to take care of him. He does know his art, even the newest painters in France and Spain, so we had delightful conversations. I just don't know what to do now. I am not being a good hostess. I am too solitary at heart."

"What should I tell him?"

"I guess I should do my duty. Get the champagne and an ice bucket with two glasses. I'll go ahead and meet up with him. Thank you, Kenal."

By the time I went out with the treats, she was standing next to him at her easel. They worked quietly side by side. Just so long as he wasn't another fisherman, using paints as bait.

That evening the table was to be full: the Lord and Lady, Euphoria, Letty, Csaba, and the Horshams. Completing the table was the Bishop, without his Fanny. They all gathered for cocktails beforehand. I watched Csaba being introduced to Lady Gladys. When he kissed her hand and praised the beauty of the grand saloon, she sparkled back. She was not used to getting such attention from visiting men, let alone any men. It was no surprise she took his arm to lead all into the dining room.

For once the service went at a slow pace because Csaba regaled all with tales of his country and family. Here is my sense of his speech.

"My ancestors developed a swath of wine grapes on the volcanic mountainside along the river Tizsa. The closest town was a crossroads, with travelers and traders from Russia to Western Europe and back. It is still a rare place, welcoming those rejected by others, such as Jews and Romani. The sidewalk coffee houses produced a symphony of languages and laughter. It is Hungarian hospitality at its best.

"And the culture! The town is small, yet the leading aristocrats studied in England. They made our little corner of the country most advanced in ideas and the arts. Before I was born, such men fought for nationalism, for freedom from Germanic control and culture. I was truly blessed to grow up in such liberal and creative society."

His eyes rolled upward while he sighed, perhaps recalling a youthful fantasy. There followed what seemed a Hungarian quotation.

"Szygami potami zboray toth...." (Obviously, I have no idea of his words and made them up here.

"Petofi," he explained. "Our great poet."

"And your family are still there?" inquired the Bishop.

"Sadly, just one, my older brother Miklos. While I was at university my parents and sister died in a riverboat accident."

"That's so sad," whispered Letty. "I cannot imagine losing my mama and papa."

Others added comments of condolence.

"I was quite bereft and wanted to quit my education, but my brother insisted I stay. You see, when we were children the vineyards suffered a terrible disease that destroyed the plants."

"Phylloxera!" piped Letty. "I read about it in my geography book."

"Phylloxera. Yes, a scourge. My father had to tear out all the vines and have the land rest for many years before it was safe to plant again. Miklos and I are just restarting. My family were on their way to Budapest to explore moving there when they died. My brother and I would not give up like so many neighbors. Most servants left, and the manor is shabby, but we enjoy life, which is the point, is it not?"

"Yet you don't stay there in Hungary. From what I hear, you flit about different countries and paint," noted the Bishop a bit tartly.

"That is true. I am a dreamer. I must create. Still, on my travels I do some business. I meet with chefs and shops and tell them our wine will be returning. I collect names for when the first bottles are ready to sail away to both Russia and the West. That is my assignment. I am a secret agent."

Lord Leo woke up. "Similar threats occurred here in the past, though they were not so devastating to our welfare. I agree, we can live well with less. Our land provides the minimum, even when nature is at her worst. We are at a time when other estates are selling out their libraries and art works, the families moving to London.

Taxes are worse than the vagaries of nature. We in Cornwall mock the extravagance of those in some other counties. Perhaps it is the weather, the winds and many days of rain, that make us conservative."

"So we are, as one, Lord Leo. No wonder I feel such comfort here."

Notice the unspoken, the benefits of two American de Loverly wives in a row. English estates where the firstborn son submitted to a Yankee bride were not moving toward decrepitude. Without finding a similar bride, the owners of magnificent Blenheim would be facing disintegration.

Bunston accompanied the men to oversee their needs in the billiard room, while I attended the ladies for sherry in the small sitting room. For once Lady Gladys joined her sex.

"Euphoria, what a delightful guest, your Mr Szarka. I hope he can stay more than a few days. I want to hear more about his many travels and the artists he knows," said Lady Gladys. "If only I were free to flit about, as the Bishop noted. You know my love of languages and sausages."

"I admit I was uncertain about his coming here, since I did not know him very long in Baden. But as you can see, he has charm that makes him hard to resist. Hungarians are a much-conquered people who have learned to live by wit and dissembling."

"So you still lack certainty? You think he may have an ulterior motive in coming here?"

"It may just be my temperament, Gladys. My independence. Since you bring it up, I hope he has no intentions with regard to me. Intimately, that is."

"It would take a most unusual man to break through your barriers. I should not worry. You always manage such situations deftly. Now I, of course, am more romantic, and enjoy his little flirtations. Do you not agree, Lady Horsham?"

"Definitely. I plan to invite him to stay over with us for a night or two. What Hungarian of his class is also not a fine rider? I know he would enjoy our stable and some dashes alongside me across the fields."

As I listened to this discussion, I did not anticipate how this stranger would change our lives.

Following several days of sunny fall weather, dark clouds and frost prevented further painting ventures outside. Csaba announced at supper that he must leave, that it was not fair to impose further on the family. Everyone looked to Lord Leo, who quickly said, "Nonsense. Our invitation stands for you to stay so long as you wish."

The others followed with a cascade of "don't goes" and "please stays."

"Naturally I am most humbly grateful for your hospitality. Nonetheless, I have my sales work to continue. I must head up to Glasgow and Edinburgh before winter arrives. I owe it to my brother."

Gladys asked, "Can you stay a few more days, until the approaching storm blows over? And promise to return one day when it is convenient during your travels."

"My dear lady, how could I not? I will stay a few more days, but alas, must double my travel plans afterward"

As I scanned the table, three in attendance appeared to be holding back tears: Lady Gladys, Letty, and Euphoria.

Csaba departed, as promised, on a bright breezy day following the storm. Lord Leo drove him to Exeter to catch a train northbound.

The household returned to its quiet, languid days. Although Lord Leo was fully healed, when the weather improved he was not one for roughing it on horseback. Euphoria announced she would stay through winter in order to tutor Letty, who was set to attend a daily lady school in Bude in the spring. Lady Gladys slinked off to spots unknown while always appearing for the evening meal. It was a calm after the storm.

To my surprise, Chippy Norton appeared.

"I thought you would be in college."

"I graduated. Lord Leo invited me back to finish my history of the family. He is intent that it include a correct account of the rumored curse."

"So you'll be needing me in the afternoons again? In your absence, I continued to arrange materials and books. I hope you don't mind. I canna enjoy being idle."

"I do see the books are finally in place according to our plans, the manuscripts all boxed up. I will find it much easier to settle down and write as a result. If I need you at all, it will be for special tasks that may arise. For now, though, you will have to find other diversions. I prefer to work alone at this stage."

His refusal did not disappoint me. I enjoyed working alone as well. The question was, what now? Truth be, Slanderley didna need the few man servants it had. Should I to speak up, then Scullion would lose his job. I could not do that, and must think of ways to ensure we were both useful.

My worries soon dissolved. The Lord's secretary, Jemima, called me into her office with surprising news. Mr Bunston would be leaving for some months to stay at a rest home. She held an invisible glass up to her lips to code the truth. That he had not been tossed out for good, she said, was due to his special place in Lord Leo's family. The distant cousin, I recalled.

This temporary departure meant temporary assignments for the male staff. I would take on Bunston's duties, and Scullion move into mine. Given Bunston hardly worked as it was, I had to ask about my new responsibilities. In addition to managing the door and guests, as well as overseeing Scullion at the formal tables, I would do some valet service. When I objected that I knew nothing about valet tasks, Jemima assured me all would go well.

Indeed, I soon learned Lord Leo was eccentric about his personal care. He had favorite clothes that he put on himself because he was squeamish about being touched by a man. Also, he slept naked and did not want to be seen in that state. When he undressed at night, he placed his soiled clothing into a crocodile suitcase left outside the door for me to deliver to the laundress. The latest Hall Boy, Diggory, handled any boots and shoes. While milord was at breakfast, the maid tidying his room, I brushed what needed brushing and tidied his shaving equipment. He had a barber in London, and was fastidious about maintaining his meagre facial hair when home.

One afternoon, I was making my daily walk through the rooms, checking for needed repairs, proper furniture placement, and such when I decided to head up to the nursery floor, which I normally ignored. There I found Letty standing behind an easel, a bowl of fruit on the table before her. The old schoolroom was where Euphoria gave her lessons, but the teacher was missing. I made loud steps not to scare her.

"Kenal. Do come in. This is my latest lesson. As you can see, I have yet to paint. I find sketching the arrangement is very difficult to get right. I am wearing my eraser to a nub."

"I admire your persistence. I canna draw anything. I write Jackdaw scribbles. Where is your aunt?"

"She has gone to London for several days to visit friends and acquire some more paint and canvases. So I am on my own. She left me some workbooks in French and biology to fill out in the afternoons. I am so stiff from standing here. Do let us sit on the longue while I relax. I hear you have a new position."

"Yes, I am temporary for Bunston, not that it is a big change. Your father is easy to please."

"I hope so. I don't see him often, but that is the way of our sort. We grow up quick on our own, if we are wise."

"I am sure you are wise, Miss Letty, for you act older than your years."

"Did you know your father?

"Yes, before he died. We all lived together in the cottage, many brothers and sisters, so we learned from one another. Me Mam taught me to weave nets and collect food from the woods. With me Tas at sea so much, I were closer to her. I were slower to grow up."

"That sounds strange, everyone in a small house on top of one another. I prefer my privacy, my rooms in the east wing away from my parents. We are all private in my family."

"So I have learned. I canna tell where one of you be most of the time."

"That is because we have secrets. I told you, remember?"

"Yes, and left me wondering, though twere not my proper place to do so. Secrets must be silent."

"Oh, no. Sometimes they are to be shared, with the right person. I shall tell you one now." She leaned in. "There is a secret staircase from my father's trophy room down into the cellar to a door outside. He can leave when he wants and no one will know. I found it one day when he was in the City."

"Once outside, he'd be seen."

"No, the door is hidden. You can try to find it sometime. You'll learn the rest of the secret."

"Miss Letty, I do not like this. I donna want to spy on your father. You are young, a time when spying can be fun, even a way to learn. But it is out of my place. Please do not mention it again."

"I do not mean to upset you Kenal, but there may come a time you need this discovery. It makes a bond between us. You don't understand now, but homes with so many secrets can be dangerous."

"The Curse again?"

"No, Kenal, real life. No magic. No curses."

A Secret Revealed

Alice ran up to me one morning, breathing heavily and jittery. "I'm going to London and Paris! I never imagined traveling beyond Exeter. We leave in two weeks. Lord Leo wants to have his leg injury checked by his Harley Street surgeon and get measured for new suits. He says he wants the latest fashion, but the truth is he has put on weight."

"That sounds wonderful, Alice. Why Paris as well?"

"Lady Gladys has read about a new style from House of Paul Poiret. Milady showed me drawings in a mode magazine. The gowns are soft and flowing, with no nasty corsets underneath, and even show the ankles, can you imagine. She'll need entirely new undergarments as well. She plans to visit old friends, so we may be there as long as a month."

"I'll miss you, Alice. What of your blacksmith?"

"Mr Tiddlysquat will just have to miss me too. But you'll have more time to read and hike. No visitors to wait on. I hear Letty will stay with the Horshams. It will be quiet as a tomb apart from mealtimes."

"Where will you stay in Paris? Does the family also have a house there?"

"Oh, no. We'll be at some ritzy hotel. Well, she'll have the fancy, while I will be in the servant section for sleep and meals. During the day I will have to carry her parcels and see to her every wish. I dare say I won't have time to explore."

"I doubt Lady Gladys will keep you that busy. I am sure other servants will be seeking companions for walks about the city. Euphoria has told me its parks are a delight. There is even a famous cemetery people like to visit. Can you imagine?"

"You may be right, Kenal. Thank you for the suggestions."

"Do send me postcards, Alice. I want to see Paris through your eyes. One day I will go to London and Paris and stay at a fancy hotel too."

"If anyone from our lowly place can do so, it will be you, Kenal. I will tempt you with scenes from the city you can hang on your wall."

So on a bright and chilly day my lordly couple left for London and, after that, milady and Alice to Frogland. Jemima posted a list of maintenance work to be done in their absence. Before starting my assignment, however, I was to accompany Letty to Cromwoh. She left her Cob behind this time because the Horshams believed she was ready to try an easygoing horse.

When Gleeves and I arrived, we turned to leave, but were invited to sup in the servant quarters. Though I had never been to Cromwoh, the rooms seemed familiar. There were the well-worn stairs to the ground floor, the flaking brown paint on the walls, and the dining table surrounded by a collection of assorted wooden chairs. Before sitting down, I looked for Dom, wishing to have a talk with him.

"Dom is no longer with us. He left several weeks ago."

"That is a surprise. He seemed to enjoy working here."

"True, he did. But he was offered a position under Lord Rashcum and took leave immediately. He didn't even say goodbye."

"That is not all," added the housekeeper. "The Lord actually picked him up in his roadster and he exited through the front door, as though he were of that class."

The tattle continued, for one of the worst crimes a servant can commit is to think about moving up class. Doing so, as Dom seems to have managed, led to unkindly talk. Soon the valued co-worker turned into an odd sort, a lay-abed, and perhaps even a thief.

"I can say one good thing," added a pretty young maid, "that he never took advantage of us ladies. He were always a gentleman with us."

Secretly envious, I spoke up at last. "I agree that Dom was always a gentleman. And when he helped us out at Slanderley, he did more than his share of work. Now I thank you, for we must get back to our duties there."

Gleeves even gave me the reins so he could smoke a wormy cigar during the drive back.

"I say, Kenal, you be right about Dom as a fine worker. You should know though that words did pass among the men about his private behavior. Lord Rashcum never married, which has led to suspicions about him. Lacking an heir, he even adopted a young cousin to inherit the estate."

"Not everyone wants to marry. I have heard of other cases like his."

"Yes, but you see we think Dom wants to take the cousin's place. Lord Rashcum has hired him as valet and general aide. He will be with the man all the time, while the cousin will be off at school."

I must say this story shocked me, though I kept my thoughts inside. "The cousin will always have the advantage of blood," I stated optimistically.

"I hope so, Kenal. With you, I prefer to trust people's good nature."

My special assignment now was to go through the formal serving ware, check it against inventory, clean and polish, and send items off for repairs. This took but a few days. I saved my favorite part for last, the monstrous centerpieces, usually silver or enameled, with places to insert candles and flowers. Many came from Lady Gladys's pre-marital purchases. They included Hindu deities in strange commingles, platypi, giant beetles with bejeweled eyes, and ebony ravens among others. They were so odd and toy-like that I made up stories as I cleaned them. This little platypus dances with the blue god, bites him, and kills him.

My duty completed, I were free to poke about the entire house, something I had never done, with Gwandror tagging along for company. Lady Gladys's writing desk held tiny drawers full of keepsakes: chicken legs, rosaries, buttons, Hungarian stamps, minute spiders with gummy webs decorating the corners. Upstairs, her sitting room revealed a cage with rabbits, opened to give them free reign of the room. Gnarl marks spoiled every furniture leg, while nails shredded the cushions. I learned Diggory was caring for the rabbits in their owner's absence. Spotting the Pudelpointer, they scurried under the four-poster, unaware he was as docile as a tortoise.

Where next? The Lord's trophy room, his preferred spot. Beneath the glassy eyes of the moth-eaten decapitations were book cases filled with custom leather-bound volumes, his large literary collection. Used to spending his days in this room, Gwandror wandered to the hearth, collapsed, and snarfled like a steam train.

Recalling Letty's story of a secret stairwell, I circled the walls in search of a possible hidden door. In time, I suspected a narrow bookcase full of mysteries and poked at its edges without success. Scanning the titles, I found Wilkie Collins's *Hide and Seek*. Pulling it out, a series of clicks and creaky wheels suggested a tumbler at work. When I pulled on the shelf, the case opened to expose a passageway. I were surprised it neither smelled dank nor was littered with webs. I lit a candle and started down the stone steps. Halfway down was a heavy oak door, iron straps nailed across to block it. Turning a corner, I saw light leak beneath a door facing the bottom step. The exit unlocked, I opened into an overgrown arbor that ran along a high wall enclosing the stable area.

A well-worn path led out to the woods, and from there to a most surprising spot, the gate house, home of Mrs Quirk and Jemima. I hid behind a tree, watching the sisters and young Eddie enjoying tea at a round table. The boy's ginger hair glowed aflame in the sunlight, reminding me without hesitation of milord. So this was behind the strange employment of the two sisters, their well-paying positions. What more than a bastard could explain the situation?

People thought me naïve, but I was not stupid. I knew of fallen women, Jezebels, and had heard of the unwed mothers who resulted. Most such women ended up begging, in poor houses, or in selling their bodies. Rarely did the father admit his role and help the sinful lass. Clearly Lord Leo was one exceptional redeemer.

I wondered whether Letty had ever taken my route and come to the same conclusion. I decided not. Her Scottish nurses would have seen to her proper upbringing as a future lady of a manor. Could she know she had a half-brother in Eddie Quirk? Or was I spinning stories from floss?

I did what anyone would in my circumstance. I sought out someone to share the tale. Twere easy to wander through the woods toward Chippy's cottage. He were enjoying tea in the sun and invited me to sit beside. Though I did not reveal the secret staircase, I did explain my thoughts about Eddie Quirk.

"I learned about this situation when I was hired," he replied. "Jemima wanted me to understand why Eddie had so much run of the place. The Quirk sisters' father and Lord Sinjin belonged to a small recorder ensemble that favored Norwegian sea shanties. Lady Peony and Lord Sinjin were very sociable and held many events for friends and their children, through which the youngsters became friends. After the girls were orphaned, Leo offered a comfort to the younger sister, Gertrude, who returned his affection.. By then, he was in University, so they met there furtively. As you know, after being orphaned, both women had employment at Crackington in nearby Devon.

"When Leo asked permission to marry Gertrude, his father objected strongly and began the search for an American heiress. A set of circumstances aided them, though not to their full wishes. Alas, she became pregnant. Lord Sinjin died before he knew about the child. Leo inherited and Euphoria came up with the plan to hire both sisters. Gladys arrived, unaware her husband's bastard lived on the grounds."

"Do you think milady knows the truth now?"

"I doubt it. She is too busy with her private schemes and religious affectations. Once Letty and Algie were born, she considered herself free from most lady duties. Her eccentricity meant Leo too had more privacy to continue his relationship."

"Does Eddie know Leo is his father?"

"No. He is too young and cannot be trusted with the knowledge. I am sure Lord Leo will see to his needs when he is older. He can never inherit, of course, which I believe would not bother him. He is bright and curious and lacks pride. He will have the best of being to the manor born, that is, the run of the estate without any of the responsibilities."

"I nae envy the titled, tied to customs and demands they may resent. A gaol of sorts."

"Some fit in well and see their birthright as a mission. Others are nincompoops, the result of so much inbreeding. Plus the usual array of the greedy, the cruel, and the egoists. Just look at the House of Lords."

"I've nae interest in Westminster. It cares not about me or my like, so I care not about it. Yet could you not be there one day."

"Yes, Kenal, as one of the more serious members, I hope. Now you must swear never to discuss your discovery. Don't even guess who else in the manor knows the truth. Any leak would destroy the family, even Slanderley itself."

Now you see why I be warming up to Norton. He treated me like I were a smart pupil. He trusted me. True, he were a nutty bird lover and knew of buggery, but I could overlook those failings.

When with him, I studied his behavior, how he moved, sat down, and gestured. He exerted minimal effort and avoided flighty moves of his hands or arms. I copied these actions, for they expressed a trait I valued highly, self-control.

The travelers returned, a second carriage following, full of parcels. Thanks to Alice's postcards, I knew the names of places she visited and could ask her about. I was right that she found time to walk out in the companionship of other servants.

"Paris was so beautiful. My postcards to you didn't lie. Still, it was often grey or drizzly, the people passing by with grim faces as though smiling were illegal. They seemed snooty and looked down on us once they saw we were visitors. Worst of all, they were French."

"You must have had some enjoyments."

"Tis true. I loved sitting outdoors in the cafes, under an umbrella even. I had coffee with milk and delicious pastries. Even then a man might come to the table to interfere. I heard about very rude shows with naked people performing in late night clubs. They have many churches but they are Roman and certainly don't obey our Scripture. I am so happy to be back."

"I am glad to see you here as well. I have grown weary of little work to do. It took me less than a week to review the formal silverware. Lady Gladys will be very pleased."

"Oh, she pleased me as well. She had too many new dresses for her wardrobe, so as I brought them in from the ironer, she insisted I take several of her everyday frocks to put in a chest toward my own wedding. The silks of her new evening dresses were smooth as rabbit fur. She could stand up to any woman in society now. I saw how women admired her as we strolled in Kensington."

While she went on about the rich fabrics and the real furs, I paid little attention. I practiced deceptive fascination. Me Mam always tsked about fancy ladies. "All one needs is a few simple bits of clothing, one for work, one for church, and a thick cloak against the storm."

Mam's voice in my mind poked me to see how even saintly Alice had her weaknesses.

Slanderley fell into its lazy period. Another winter were coming, and milady decided she could save her fancy gowns for spring, so few guests appeared, only milord's closest friends. Letty and Euphoria kept to the east wing, Leo in the trophy room, and Gladys who-knew-where. Bunston returned, though we suspected he was still into nips.

One blustery November night, just as all were heading to bed, a most unexpected guest appeared. I was checking the doors were locked, when an explosive sound on the front entry stairs startled me, along with everyone else. Being first at the door, I opened it to find a roadster crashed onto the stone steps. *Thelma.* She were bloodied and moaning from hitting her face into the steering wheel. When I tried to help her out, it was clear her right leg were injured as well.

Lord Leo were close behind. "Thelma, what in God's good name are you doing here at this time of night?"

She said nothing while I aided her, limping up the steps.

Lady Gladys pushed her husband aside. "Don't just crutch her. Lift her up and place her in the small saloon. Where is Bunston? That lout. Get moving, Kenal."

I be large, but so too were Thelma, so I groaned as I lifted her into my arms. She nibbled my ear.

"Leo, do something. Fetch the doctor. Now!"

I had never seen milady so in charge. Her American training, I supposed. A good time to be loud and bossy.

Soon the room filled with women—Gladys, Euphoria, Letty, and Mrs Quirk. They all wanted to know why Thelma appeared in so tumultuous a manner.

"I was dining with the Tronek sisters in Bude and missed the turnoff to Pennididdle in the dark. No moon tonight, you know. Then I saw someone close behind, following me in a dark saloon car."

Mrs Quirk placed warm pads over Thelma's bruises. "That must have been a fright. At least you weren't tossed out of the auto."

"Yes, it has been so dreadful since Harry's death. Then I remembered Slanderley. By taking the entrance, I stifled the stalker, who drove on. As I was making the circular at the entry, I hit the gas instead of the brakes. So here I am, alas." She wrung her hands a bit too. "Oh, I am feeling faint. I am seeing spots. Oh, do help me!"

"Just lie back, Thelma. We'll take care of you. Mr Iliac is coming." said Lady Gladys.

I caught Euphoria's eyes, and received a tiny smirk. True, Thelma were injured, but her story seemed suspicious. We could not imagine her dining with the Tronek spinsters, a home with no males. Letty, of course, took it all in and went over to smooth Thelma's forehead.

Lady Gladys continued her ordering. "When you are patched up, you must come to our best guest suite, next to mine. Mrs Quirk, please see to that arrangement immediately. Letty, off to bed. Euphoria and I will take over. Kenal, go have cook prepare a small tea."

"Perhaps some whisky too?" peeped Thelma.

Mr Iliac arrived, examined her privately, and announced she had only minor bruises and sprains. "She should be able to return home in a day or two. Too bad about the car, fine specimen that."

Not to be thwarted, Thelma became the uninvited guest. With Bunston's return, I no longer had reason to go near the west wing, which saved me humiliating encounters with her there. Furthermore, she was no longer my mistress and could not order me up to help her.

To my surprise, Thelma were well-behaved the first few days, and spent her time "recovering" from her fright. Having done so, she finally appeared at dinner one evening.

"I am so grateful for your hospitality, my Lord."

"It is my dear wife you should thank. She oversaw all the comforts for you these past few days."

"Now that I am here, I was wondering whether you might show me about the stables and advise me on buying a horse or two."

"I thought you didn't ride."

"Not yet, but perhaps you could give me some pointers."

"You really need a teacher for that. I am known to be one of the best riders in the region, but I do not have the temperament to teach." (A good escape there, I considered.)

Gladys smiled and suggested, "Would you like to see my latest Parisian purchases? I would love to guide you for when you go there to shop."

"I prefer to sketch my own clothes and made bespoke in London. In America, my dresses attracted the most exciting newspaper coverage. At the Astor ball, I wore a dress of puce silk, the skirt eight-foot around, a battery tucked inside to light up my vaulted bosom. Everyone talked about it."

"I'm sure they did. Yet you may get ideas by going to the couturiers. I can get you in, since you have never done so. Meanwhile, come to my suite tomorrow to see my beauties. My favorite actually has slacks, though very wide to give the appearance of a skirt. And they require no corset to destroy your lungs."

This prattle continued to the end of the meal. As he passed by me, Lord Leo muttered what seemed to be "Can no one rid me of her?"

Sure enough, Thelma continued to intrude upon Lord Leo with this or that suggestion. He could show her the gardens, such as they were. He could drive her to the moors to see where Harry died. He could teach her to down-shift. She wore long flowing scarves, and I suspected, given his facial expressions, that he wanted to garrote her with one.

One day she appeared in a Poiret gown, obviously from milady's wardrobe. She overflowed it to reveal almost all her grand bosom. By the end of the meal some seams were opening. Poor Lady Gladys.

The days passed, and you don't need to hear any more. I know you are wondering who will be die next. So I shall get on with the plot.

It were a ferociously windy day, a Sunday so horrible that no one went to church or chapel. Lacking gas warmth in the east wing, Letty and Euphoria camped in the small saloon, huddled by its perky hearth. We servants huddled in the kitchen, where Mrs Viscous kept a spit going and the ovens at full blast. The de Loverlys and Thelma remained in their suites, and requested meals be delivered to them accordingly.

We could hear tree limbs crack and tumble nearby, and gave thanks we didna have to be outside. I hoped the grounds workers were safe and secure in their tiny cottages. After supper, Mr Bunston brought out some of his special spirits and invited us to join in. I were tempted, for he said they warmed the belly, but I kept true to my beliefs. A kind of party followed. I were surprised to see Alice take a sip and snuggle next to Turgid. True, I were jealous, even though I were too young to court her. I asked God's forgiveness that I sinned in my mind.

The heat making me sleepy, I retired earlier than usual to my comfortable, windowless room next to Mr Bunston's. I crawled right under my feather quilt without removing my day clothes. I think there is a god or goddess who brings the night's release, but I can't recall the name. Anyway, it whispered in my ears, and I was quick out of reality.

Toward morning, when dreams most announce themselves, I found myself running, running, running from some unseen attackers. My heart pounded like a snare drum, my legs sore from the effort. The sky were a strange maroon, with sea-colored clouds obscuring a full moon. The stars, large and bright orange, danced in between. An odor of decay surrounded me, like coming upon a rotting deer carcass in the woods.

I opened me mouth to scream, yet nothing came out. My lungs felt aburst, threatening my collapse. Then I saw the hedgehog folly and beat upon the door in its rear. My fists sprouted blood as I hammered away. The hedgehog structure came alive, swaying and gribbling strange noises. The door did not open. The pursuer caught up, for I felt talons clawing down my back, a stream of bloody liquid in tow.

I awoke, sweaty as in shock. My legs ached, my hands bound in tight fists. Feeling for a match, I lit the bedside candle and went to my mirror. I were relieved to see me back in my full corporeal form. Then I laughed that a dream could so upset me. Oh, Kenal, I said aloud, you have nae to fear.

That morn, the furious bluster continued. Mr Bunston advised us to stay indoors. The laundress had an unexpected free day, so she taught me how to make soap. At lunch, Alice returned with the full breakfast tray she had taken to Lady Gladys's sitting room.

"I suppose she was not hungry. She is like that some days, but this is twice in a row. I'm sure she'll enjoy the next meal I am taking up."

"I thought wealthy Americans like to be fat," noted Diggory. "I have seen their photos in the used magazines she leaves for me to deposit. Some resemble walruses, all blubbery and toothy in fancy gowns."

"Perhaps that is why she did not fit into that society," suggested Alice. "She has always made a point of staying thin, even to fasting entire days now and then. But who are we to say, except Mrs Viscous, who works so hard to satisfy."

"Thank ye, Alice. I do disappoint when a full tray returns. She could let me know ahead of time."

"Her slim figure made her perfect for the new Parisian style. Mr Poiret delighted how his draping flowed over her body. Thelma would look good in them as well, except they would show off her muscular arms."

"Speaking of Thelma," I intervened, "how is she managing through all this recent isolation?"

The under-maid replied, "She has a tremendous appetite. I can barely manage the tray. I suppose she is finding some entertainment in her rooms. I never see her."

At dinner, Alice returned another full tray. "I don't think milady even took it in. It must be a fast day."

That night the weather calmed, the sun blared, the air sent a cuddly warmth. Mr Bunston ordered the personal servants to check on their charges. Of course, someone was missing, *Lady Gladys.*

Lord Leo noted he'd had no communication with her since they went into their separate rooms two nights previous. He said he welcomed the complete quiet so he could read the pile of novels in his room. Thelma explained she took the time for long naps in between writing letters, how she was behind in thanking those who consoled her over Harry's death.

We went out in search of milady, and soon enough found her body all akimbo at the bottom of the cliff. In fact, I were the first who found her. At least her face was not visible, so I had no glassy eyes to haunt me afterwards.

I called out for others to see the sad result. As each arrived and peered down, questions as to Lady Gladys's fate arose. Why she went out during the gale to the cliff side was a puzzle. She wore a long fur coat over her winter night gown, with heavy rubber boots on her feet. She knew the pathway well. We most agreed with Mr Bunston's guess that a sudden gust threw her off balance and over. Though why was she out at all, and there of all places?

Lord Leo finally arrived to review the scene. He ordered Gleeves to fetch both a constable and the Mr Iliac. Though his face remained tight against tears, his legs and fingers tremored in what—fury? grief? anger? I quietly asked whether I could do anything. He told me to alert Euphoria, who was in the nursery with Letty.

Lady Gladys were dead, a reality that blocked any "if only" musings. Snerd and Turgid took on the task of recovering her body and placing it in the main saloon.

Upstairs, I found a painting lesson in progress. Catching Euphoria's eye, I nodded at her to come into the hallway, where I explained the terrible situation. I watched as Euphoria passed on the tragic news with as much gentleness as possible. Letty fell into her aunt's arms, inconsolable. Despite seeing her mother only briefly each day, it were clear Letty loved her fully. I thought of me Mam, how much worse her loss would be for me, her apron hanger-on.

After leaving, I began to shudder and sob as well. Lady Gladys had trusted me like few in my life. She hinted at secrets in her marriage and her Summer House activities. Somewhere, perhaps in America, she had become interested in Roman Catholic ways, and was creating a path toward, dare I think, a nunnery? That would be a terrible blot on the family.

Composing myself, I returned to the main floor, to see the authorities had arrived. Constable Mustard was giving his report to Lord Leo, accompanied by Jemima, Mrs Quirk, Thelma, and Mr Bunston. I stood ready by the door.

"I note the corpus was moved into the manor before I could study the scene in its fullness. Nonetheless, I did a thorough search of the area where the tragic event initiated. I saw nothing unusual to raise suspicions. The wind-gusts had swept the walkway clean, so no footprints appeared. A minor erosion above suggests loose dirt may have tripped her. The nights being very dark, she may just have lost her bearings. She likely hit her head on an outcrop just below, then tumbled further. In addition, I cannot imagine anyone from this noted family, nor its faithful servants, enact a criminal deed. Based on such evidence, I shall conclude my report as death by accident."

"Thank you, Constable," said milord. "I appreciate your succinct summary and look forward to your Coroner's testimony."

The constable bowed and exited the room backwards. I saw him out and returned to the mourners. Mrs Quirk had moved to sit beside Lord Leo on a sofa and hold his hand. Thelma was smoking and staring at the two.

"Jemima and I will see to the services, Leo. The family chapel, I presume."

"Yes, but not the Bishop. She had a rosary in her coat pocket. I have known for some time that she was planning to convert to the Romans. Her secret friends included nuns from Plimsoll Abbey, whose robes she copied and kept in the summer house. She knew I disapproved, alas, yet she was determined to have her way. I feared she wanted to convert the children as well."

Thelma stood and walked over to him. Placing a hand on his shoulder, she moaned, "I also honor your wishes, Lord Leo. We know your relationship was not always easy, so—"

"Stop! She was my wife, the mother of my children. We had little in common, yet she did her duty. Do not speak ill of her. She was a stranger in a strange land, and I was not the most sympathetic husband. I owe her the ritual she would want."

The room sat silent until the Mr Iliac came with his account for Lord Leo.

"I have completed my sad inspection, and appreciate the care with which the men brought her up. They did no further harm in the process. I shall keep this short. It appears she fell two nights ago, during the height of the gales. She died from skull fractures, instantaneous. Had she survived, the further injuries would have left her paralyzed, a terrible fate for such a healthy and active woman."

"Though no death be good, doctor, it is a relief to me she did not suffer. That is what so worried me when I gazed upon her battered form. We all wish an easy death, no? Being pious, I doubt she feared death, yet hers was graced."

At that point, Thelma fainted.

"Bunston, take care of that damned woman," milord said as he left the room.

An hour later, the clatter of suitcases bouncing on the main stairs preceded a similarly noisy Thelma, stomping to announce her departure. Gleeves took her away in an open stable cart as though off to the guillotine.

During suppers the following days, we servants admitted to little knowledge of her ladyship, all except Alice. She added little, beyond praise for the woman's easy care. Being so independent, Lady Gladys refused many expected personal tasks, such as helping her into underwear or attaching her jewelry. We missed her presence, certainly, yet most held no special affection for her. It were to others like losing a distant aunt.

Rather, our concern was Lord Leo, how he would handle being a widower. Though he grieved many hours in his trophy room, he turned his attention to his children. Consulting with Euphoria, he allowed Algie to join the family table now. I hoped his father would provide the guidance the Scots ladies had failed to accomplish. The lad seemed less affected by the death of his mother, which only upset Letty more. Those dinners were silent as a flat sea.

The morning of the service, we servants formed a row of silent crows in the last pews. Bishop Wurzel oversaw a brief service consisting mostly of prayers and hymns. At the end, Lord Leo stood up to announce a second service would follow. He had promised such to his wife, and those who disapproved were welcome to leave without guilt. Most of the gentry, alert to the addition, shuffled out with him. We in service remained out of curiosity.

To my surprise, a Catholic priest entered to perform a funeral mass service hard to watch. So much mumbo-jumbo and irritating incense. The priest from St Peter's in Bude wore gold-embroidered vestment, an immodest insult to modest Jesus. Two Abbey nuns sat upfront and joined loudly in the responses while rattling their beads. As we left, they wailed and stayed behind by the crypt.

Once Lady Gladys departed to the holy realm, I saw no more glimpses of nuns about the follies.

A minor shock followed, for the coroner's inquest did not conclude as expected.

First, Inspector Termagant criticized his constable's conclusions. On the stand, he testified, "Lack of evidence is not evidence that nothing mischievous occurred. My constable did not do a thorough investigation. His belief no one at the manor could commit a crime reveals his weakness. I fear he let the class superiority of the family color his approach. He forgot justice requires a blind eye to such distractions. Her ladyship could, for example, have come upon a nefarious trespasser."

The Mr Iliac followed with new information as well. "When I had more leisure with the body, I discovered two torn fingernails. Perhaps they were from clutching at the cliff while she fell, yet I found no evidence of stone or plant material underneath. I cannot conclude she fell on her own until we have more information."

The conclusion was "insufficient evidence" to attribute the cause of death.

Milord mumbled as he left the hearing, Euphoria at his side whispering responses. That a murderer could be in the neighborhood or in the manor itself struck me and others dumb. A woman dead in her prime. No one mentioned the Curse.

Lord Leo immediately set the house for a traditional year's mourning. We had already draped some windows with black, and turned mirrors to the wall. He cancelled a small ball Lady Gladys had arranged to celebrate the arrival of springtime. The only social activities would be informal suppers with his closest friends, no more than four guests, and very seldom.

Euphoria worried about Letty's state of mind within such a dark and dour household. She decided the best solution was for the two of them move to the town home in London, from which the girl could walk to a fine Day School. After a long discussion, milord agreed.

Twas a sad day when I saw the two off in the carriage to the train terminal. I knew, however, that Euphoria would be a good foster mother to Letty, just as she had been to Lord Leo when their parents died in his childhood.

Protecting Algie was more difficult. Lord Leo did not want a tutor moving into the household. Nor did he think the boy ready for a boarding school. After some consultation, he arranged for Chippy Norton to take Algie to live in Oxford at the Norton family manor and tutor him there.

Alice desired to marry as soon as possible. With no mistress to assist, she was losing her favourite part of her charge. She hoped her blacksmith had saved enough that she could leave service within a few months to join him.

"If I'm to be just a maid, I'd rather be me own."

Following the inquest, men from the Bude police force came to explore every inch of the scene and interview those residing on the estate at the time. Given we had each been so isolated in separate rooms during the storm, no one had an alibi, which meant everyone had one. Frustrated, the inspector brought in a climbing hobbyist to scour the cliffs for anything unusual. That proved successful, for he came up the ropes with a bedraggled ladies glove. When they took it around the manor, several people said it looked familiar, but they could not spot the source. Perhaps it belonged to a woman visitor who dropped it long ago? The policemen questioned that possibility, for the fabric seemed of recent vintage.

The identification moved forward when the Slanderley laundress Tabitha recalled it coming in with a small bundle during the auto rally gathering. Time passed while the investigation led to interviewing the few women who had visited that event. Several women guests recalled who wore the glove, which had unusual colors and rare Belgian lace. The owner even flaunted her hands around to belittle their own simpler ones.

The police repeatedly heard, "It belonged to that Grubb woman. She was none too kind regarding Lady Gladys either. She had her eyes on Lord Leo."

Satisfied they had found the killer, the police went to Pennididdle to arrest Thelma, and found her missing from the manor. Myope, a near-blind caretaker, said he had not heard her shuffling about the manor for days. Rumors followed. I had no doubt she had hooked yet another victim.

The Slanderley Curse

Midsummer Folly

It be about my fifth year at Slanderley, and a most dour year it were. With the children gone, and Lord Leo cradling his grief in private, the staff puttered around making work. By the end of three months, every piece of metal shone as if new, every fabric cleared of dust or stain.

I served the same table of guests. They were the Bishop and Fanny Wurzel or the Bude Grimaces.. Fanny Wurzel moved into Lady Gladys's head seat, which matched her sense of superiority. Without my late ladyship's management, the plates arrived at a turtle's pace, which allowed Fanny to chew all her food and avoid another choking collapse. One time milord invited the Tronek spinsters, who so competed with one another for his attention that he never asked them back.

The meals were fully Cornish, for milord was never one for what he called "gastronomics." He could have lived all day on pasties. Mrs Viscous was pleased because she could prepare batches of dishes ahead of time and reheat them as needed. As a consequence, I decided to spend more time in the kitchen garden, as well as join Gleeves on trips to the nearby fishing ports. We all benefitted from the simpler yet filling plates.

With no large events planned, we'd no need of day workers. The only one who appeared regularly were the blacksmith, Alice's beloved. Lord Leo thought this a good time to have all the metal works, the carriages and horse implements, repaired and improved. His roadster began to rust in its shed.

When he was on the estate, Mr Tiddlysquat joined the servant table. As expected, he were a brawny sort, with permanently reddened face and arms scarred from burns. He shaved his head for comfort under a thin cap. His appetite were grand too, and included a full pitcher of cider just for hisself. Mrs Quirk made Alice sit apart from him because they had yet a formal announcement to wed.

I could see why Alice liked him. He were kindly and polite to all of us. Did I to pass by his shed, he'd call me in for a chat. I couldn't imagine doing his labor, with its sweating creeks down his body by the heat of the furnace. He said he enjoyed controlling the ore, shaping it into practical things. The day he left, he gave me a walking stick, the round black knob a perfect fit for me when poking in the animal trapped woods. He said it were to thank me for being like a brother to Alice.

Alice's presence stirred my own desires for a girl to woo. This discovery led to brain confusion and more physical frustrations. A key problem were my work. My only hope of a future wife must be one in service, so we could work together. Chapel were the likely source of a romance, yet none of the few young women there drew me like bee to pollen. I'd seen one Slyme Gurney maiden who smiled at me and almost drew me over, but she were not pious, so I heard.

This quandary continued, until I considered ways I could find a better occupation. I could continue to advance to become a butler some years in the future. I could study instruction books to become a clerk, which would lead me to life in a city. Neither of these satisfied my preference to live in nature. I were fortunate Slanderley offered me much of that enjoyment. If only the fish stock had not failed, I would take my savings and head back to Mousehole.

I shared my thoughts with Jemima one afternoon.

"I am feeling trapped betimes that I canna fulfil my manhood. It is not Slanderley, for I find many benefits here. Yet I am insecure as to my needs for the future."

"I sympathize with you, Kenal. Here I am, a spinster, also isolated from finding a possible husband. My sister and I live comfortably, and Lord Leo is an easy master. Yet I do not want to grow grey and wrinkly here. It would be a contented though limited life."

"So you do see. I think of Lady Gladys, her stories of her travels, her crossing the ocean, her trips to Paris. I have not yet been to Exeter, let alone Bath or Oxford or London. All I know is this tiny poke of land attached to England."

"I have travelled a bit more," she replied, "yet I too get wanderlust. I suspect it is less about travel than about unmet hopes. We read stories of adventure to forget our real desires."

"So do ye see no doorway, no exit?"

"I do, Kenal. The world is changing so rapidly. It is not just the new machines and cheaper printing and faster travel. It is new ideas challenging old concepts. It is history, Kenal, that will open a door.

We have seen signs in the aristocrats that have had to sell off their valuables, even tear down their manors. The working man is finding new ease in his life. It is possible Slanderley will no longer exist in a couple of decades, yet we will benefit despite its fall."

"I think I understand. The Bible tells of people in similar situations, blocked and suffering—at least we don't suffer. Then something beyond their reach brings what we call grace, blessed new choices. Such people often have to travel and struggle, but they find their place of salvation. I needs return to those stories."

"Such wise words, Kenal. For me, I put faith in King Eddie, for his optimism is leading to a time of peace and prosperity. I trust in the future overall."

Of course I were too busy with my work and the extra time to enjoy the company of my fellow servants to chew often on my predicament. Some evenings we sang folk tunes or hymns, while the grounds men played cards. Other times we told stories, true or imagined, to entertain ourselves. Diggory frightened us with his stories told in the dark, of flesh-eating monsters or poisonous snakes. Tis strange how being scared into shrieks can leave one relaxed afterwards. I now felt myself midst a new family, cousins and uncles and aunts of sorts.

Being Slanderley, something unexpected must interrupt the calm. It came with a loud banging on the heavy oak front door and ringing of the bell, a most unnecessary addition. Bunston were off somewhere with Lord Leo, so I took charge.

"See here," I shouted—."

A familiar form from the past stood face to my face.

"*Jó napot*, Mr Kenal. I had an unexpected call on a business in Portugal and thought I would cross the sea to surprise Euphoria."

Without letting him enter, I replied, "You haven't heard? Lady Gladys died. Lady Euphoria and Letty moved to London for the nonce. We are in deep mourning and not accepting visitors."

Stepping backward, he almost lost his balance. "Dead? I cannot believe this. Lady Gladys was so young and vital. Tell me you make a joke."

"Sorry, it is true. Worse, she was murdered. By Thelma Grubb."

Now he did fall backward down the steps. "Help, I think I injured my knee."

This was just what the household needed. Another uninvited guest requiring recuperation. And a mad Hungarian—or are all Hungarians mad? Alice thought so.

Mrs Quirk had heard our conversation and came to the rescue. She took one side, I the other, to hoist Csaba to the small sitting room and rest on a chaise longue. She sent Diggory to have Gleeves bring the doctor.

"Oh, my leg. I cannot bear it. Do you have some whisky?"

So much for thinking about the late Lady Gladys. I prepared a glass while Mrs Quirk arranged the pillows around his head.

"Shush," she whispered. "All will soon be well."

"You are too kind. I had a premonition not to visit. The seas were so rough I lost my supper. *Jo*, such good whisky. I think I sleep."

Mr Iliac arrived to confirm Csaba must rest until his torn ligaments healed. We forgot to inform Lord Leo, who learned of the invalid only the next day.

"That damned artist has returned? Didn't he know Euphoria was not here?"

"No, sir. He said he travels too much for any regular correspondence. Apparently he has been mostly on the Continent since seeing us."

"Mrs Quirk, send a telegram immediately to Euphoria to alert her of the damned gypsy's appearance."

"Sir, should we worry her, Letty as well? We have our ways of encouraging him to leave. Mrs Viscous can prepare some bland meals. He is a gastronome, you know, and will suffer under porridge and bland white fish."

"At least he is bedridden. As soon as he can perambulate, send him to the Slyme Gurney Inn. He is not welcome as my guest. Blasted man! Do what you can, and I agree, keep Euphoria out of it."

We arranged to bed him in the Garlic room, an east wing box room converted years ago into a guest room for less desired visitors. Lacking windows, it held a lumpy bed and offered only candle light. Its meagre loo held a noisy cistern and tiny washbasin.

We did not realize how congenial Csaba would find this poor abode. Being on the road so much, he was accustomed to noisy guest houses, even sharing rooms with fellow salesmen. He was used to gristled meat and mealy cakes.

"So charming, and no need to walk a long hallway to wash my face. This fits a prince. I kiss your hands, so to speak. But tell me about the unfortunate Lady Gladys."

I did so, soon sending him in tears.

"I apologize for being sentimental. It is the advantage of being Hungarian, to show one's heart. I know you English do not approve. Before I leave, you must show me her tomb so I can speak to her one last time."

I should like to say he proved a demanding guest, but quite the contrary. He was always apologizing or offering compliments for service, for bland food, for vinegary wine. How could I resist bringing him art materials from the nursery? He sketched me, all triangles and ovals. His gypsy spell took over each of us who dealt with him.

Mr Ileac sent a day nurse over to massage Csaba's leg and administer his pills. As a result, he felt ready to walk within a week. When told he could enjoy a room in Slyme Gurney, he actually bubbled with pleasure. I offered to accompany him to Lady Gladys's tomb while Gleeves brought the carriage over to take him off to the village.

As we were going down the main staircase, the unimaginable happened. Csaba slipped and fell, this time a cracking sound from the healthy leg. We each knew at once he faced a long rehabilitation. And so it was.

"No, milord. The doctor says travel could make matters worse. And we proved such capable hosts that we were better than a medical ward."

"Bloody hell. When I think of him, I remember his hanging all over Gladys, his hand kisses, his entreaties. She wanted to visit him in Tokaj, you know. Just keep him out of my sight."

"That is easy, sir, with him in the east wing and you being on the other side. He cannot leave his bed for some weeks. The doctor is arranging both day and night nurses to see to his most intimate needs."

"And on my accounts, no doubt. How convenient."

I did not express my disagreement. Both falls were genuine accidents. Truth is, Csaba's appearance added variety to evening table talk. Alice, Jane, and even the scullery maid vied to deliver his food and shine in his unending poetic praise. ("Your cheeks are like apricots. I kiss your hand.") We gave the nurses the adjoining Gherkin suite to use for their meals and occupation while he rested.

A week later, more excitement arrived in the form of Euphoria and Letty. Despite being sworn to secrecy, Jemima had loosened her tongue. I think she understood their presence would speed Csaba's recovery, and it seemed to prove so.

Euphoria insisted he be moved to the Prune suite, where light and fresh air flourished. She set up still life arrays on a large table and joined him in sketching and painting. When done with her studies, Letty read poetry aloud to him. Apart from breakfast, the aunt and niece took their meals in his company. None were surprised when large chests full of Tokaj wine appeared, followed by merry making in the invalid's suite.

The mourning broke prematurely, for apart from Lord Leo, the life of ease returned to the manor. He isolated himself as much as possible. Assigned to serve him, alone in the vast dining room, I stood accompanied by a symphony of grunts, grumbles, and spoon banging. Lacking a companion, he piled his mail, old newspapers, and advertising brochures in a wall around him, and insisted nothing be moved.

By spring, Euphoria convinced her brother that the mourning period must end. Given the intervening period of maintenance, the manor was in shipshape form and ready to show off.

"Brother, I've been thinking it is time to welcome more guests again. Gladys loved celebrations, so we do not dishonor her by having one similar to the last May Day event. She was so happy that day. What do you think?"

"I don't know, dear Nan. There were so many people that day. I am not ready for a crowd, nor for a loud band and children's games."

"I do understand, Leo. I know how difficult this time has been for you. On the other hand, we're not ready for a fancy dinner and costume ball either. If only we could find a compromise."

Letty followed up. "Papa, I know what we can do. Let's celebrate the Solstice. I have always wanted to attend a Solstice night. Aren't I old enough?"

"I daresay you are, Letitia. I have heard only sterling reports from your school in London. But who to invite?"

"The people who would come to a ball, but perhaps only half as many. Our usual favorite dinner guests and a few others," suggested Euphoria. "We start after dark with a late meal on the lawn."

"What would we do until dawn, Auntie? Do we just rest on carpets and nap?"

"No, dear. We can have subdued music, a flute and fiddle perhaps, leading folk songs. There'll be a bonfire, where some tell stories of long ago. We'll make flower crowns and give thanks to nature. It is a time for close friends to join together without a lot of bother."

"It is," added Leo, "founded on our ancient people, who set up the stone rings about the land. The promise of rebirth through the arrival of light. Not unlike our Easter."

I weren't so sure about that. Solstice is a pagan ritual, encouraged by a revival of the ancient ways of those who call themselves Druids. Tis heresy, pure and simple. It replaces the words of Our Lord with nature-worship. Easter as a replacement! I could only hope no Druids would appear at the event.

Days later, Mrs Quirk announced a surprise. Once the Solstice buffet was set, she welcomed, indeed encouraged us to join in the midsummer celebration. This was a reward for our fine behavior during the period of mourning. Given the guests were most familiar with the oddity of Slanderley, they would not be surprised by our participation. Indeed, the invitations included a suggestion that they bring favoured staff of their own along to join our merry servant crew.

"Not that you will mingle with gentry, of course. Daily workers will construct everything, the guest tent and a separate one for you."

Mr Bunston groaned. "Such a break in custom. I don't think I can participate."

"You must take the key welcoming role. Whether you party with your fellow workers is really up to you."

"But what do we wear?" asked Jane, the lower maid. "We don't have fancy party clothes."

"It isn't a formal event. Think outdoors, comfort clothes. The grounds men can wear their usual work coveralls. Be sure to bring shawls or coats, for it will be cold just before dawn."

"Be there whisky?" piped Sloth?

"I can't say, but I expect you all to keep on best behavior."

"That means, bring your own drink. Whisky for the posh tent only, no doubt," he mumbled.

"Turgid, I know you have a strong voice. I hope you will step up to the folk singing. And bring your tin whistle, Gleeves."

When Mrs Quirk departed, most agreed that this invitation was not a gift, for all the preparations would leave us exhausted. I kept silent about my disapproval of heathen ways, and hoped to find a spot away from all the noise for bedding down.

The night of the celebration arrived. For once the Cornish weather beast cooperated with a dry evening. I wore my raggedy travel suit, which was thick and warm. I soon met up with Mrs Viscous, buried under layers of skirts and a green knitted shawl.

"Let us watch the guests arrive," she said. "I know it is a small group."

Arrayed in his newest buttling suit, Bunston pointed people parking in the drive to walk down a carpeted lamp-lit path toward the backside of the lake. First to arrive were the Bude Grimaces, he dressed like Robin Hood, she a Maiden Marion. (They seem to have lost the theme of the holiday.) Lord Leo wore a mix of hunt costume and tweeds. Euphoria's dress was of many colored flowers, while Letty, allowed for only the supper, pranced in an orange and yellow "sun" dress. The guest meal tent was soon full with the clack of talk and the clatter of plates. (I want to say "tintabulations," but resist.)

Noticeably absent were the Bishop and Fanny Wurzel. At least they had sense to refuse such unChristian ways. The other was our invalid, Csaba, who remained in the manor with his night nurse. Mr Ileac had been concerned of late that the patient may have an internal infection from one of his broken bones.

I stood a bit outside the guest tent to watch the rituals of greeting, clinking, and gorging. As people mixed, they made those weird air kisses above each other's cheeks. The Spinster Tronek sisters entered last and waddled right up to milord. Their bodies wiggled and bounced within their robes of a white lustrous fabric. I have always thought of them as Tweedledum and Tweedledee, and nearly laughed aloud at their resembling my imagination. Noticing their intrusion on his lordship, Mrs Grimace swept in and whooshed them off for wine. Letty and Euphoria sat at a table for two, heads nose to nose, ignoring the others.

Though exempt from work, the grounds men took over the bon fire by erecting large logs in a pyramid shape over small twigs and hay. Having heard sacrifices were part of Druidism, Tabitha, our laundress, stuck a corn doll she had woven atop, dubbing it Old Hag Winter. Snerd lit the pile, causing flames to explode a fountain of sparks that forced those nearby to run out and move their carpets farther toward the woods.

I checked the small servants' tent, where our usual evening meal spread upon a rough, uncovered table. So much for a gift. Though there was no whisky, small kegs held mead and ale. Alice came over to point to the small bottles filled with homemade ginger beer. "No alcohol there, I think," she noted. "Mrs Viscous wanted to be sure we refusers had good quaffs as well."

"Nice and spicy, just the way I like it. Would you like to join me on my carpet while we eat? I have brought a couple of pails to upend for stools."

We loaded our plates with different pasties, saffron buns, and berry pie. The food being heavy, we sat quietly while ragtag musicians played in the background. They started with some jigs to alert the crowd. When they started a waltz, some of our workers coupled up to dance.

Not being a dance, I did not invite Alice to partner me. She seemed contented to sit and watch the others. We saw Letty do a spin with the Horsham's son, Reggie, who escorted her away afterward.

"Letty is off for a fortnight of riding at Cromwoh. She is ready for a full-sized mount, and they have several for her to try out," Alice whispered. "Although he is much older than her, I foresee a coupling years from now."

"Letty is still a child. Surely marriage is not on her mind," I worried.

"She knows the limitations of her position. Marriage is often on her mind, at least so far as preparing to be mistress of a manor is concerned. Lady Schools are less interested in geometry than preparation of a banquet menu."

"Yet she is such a promising artist. Could she not turn out like Euphoria, a life without a partner and pursue her creativity?"

"She will have no funds. Euphoria was fortunate to inherit from her American mother, who set up a separate account when she was born. Lady Peony disapproved of the English system and its first-son approach. Letty must keep her horizon narrow."

"You are similarly limited."

"Not really, Kenal. When I wed, I can also help my husband with his business. And I will be free to join in village affairs."

"How goes your plans? I did enjoy meeting your proposed."

"A few more months, I think, we'll have the funds. He was pleased to know none of the guest valets would be here tonight. The botherings, you know. At least you men don't have to deal with such attempts on oneself."

Little did she know. "I thought Mugwatch was your botherer, that all those insults left with him."

"Oh, no! It was Vermin, Lord Furbbelow's valet. He was always following me around and cornering me when they visited. I had to plead illness during the auto rally to escape his nasty hands and lips. That only sent him onto poor Tabitha."

Our conversation ended when Snerd joined the musicians to lead folk songs. Alice and I joined in with loud voices.

We stood up when they began "Lamorna." Even the family guests wandered over and we all sang as one chorus, proud Cornish, no matter one's social standing.

Alice had a sweet voice to join my baritone. We continued to join in other melodies.

"I took my honey home last night,

Beneath the spreading pine;

I placed my arms around her waist,

And pressed her lips on mine."

I felt myself drawn to her, leaned in, and almost kissed her. When Alice did not push me away, I stopped myself and tripped forward.

"So sorry, Alice. I didna mean—"

"I should be sorry, Kenal."

"I think we have been tricked. The ginger beer has taken over our heads. I respect you fully, you know."

"And me of you as well. It is time I joined the other maids anyway. Be sure to drink some water to wash away the vile ginger. Good solstice!"

"And to you," I replied, as I sprawled on the carpet alone. I felt Puck spread dust on my eyes, for were he not the trickster of the noted midsummer play? Falling asleep, I didna expect to wake up in the woods, an ass. I had already proved myself one.

Drifting in and out of slumber, I listened to sounds of others heading into the woods, no fairies calling them in. From deep within came sudden laughs, playful screams, and noises like fox vixens in heat.

I jerked to a hand grasping my shoulder. "Get up, Kenal. Don't miss the ceremony." Snerd pulled me upright and led me to the other grounds men. "We've planned a treat for everyone."

I heard the musicians were now further off and turned to see them at the entrance of the manor, where they began a march. Behind them, coming down the stairs, was a kind of float being carried by the village workers. As it approached, I saw it was Csaba's bed, him propped within, dressed in golden robes, his hat radiating spikes like sun rays. He waved and blessed us as though a king. White flowers flowed over his bed cover, while corn dolls and reedy farm animals flounced about his bed frame.

The parade led the float to the front of the bonfire, now in full blast thanks to new wood. Except for those sighing in the woods, everyone gathered around. Csaba's eyes glowed like coals while he peered at us. Snerd and Turgid helped sit him up to address us.

"Friends, Celts, and non-countrymen. Lend me your souls. Soon the sun deities and angels will grace us with their solstice blessings. As for me, a glass will do! All join in with me! I would say "to your health" in Hungarian, but you would think I was choking. Nevertheless, "*Egészségére!*""

"Check your rear," toasted Sloth, for reasons I did not understand.

Not a bad attempt, I thought. Next I knew, someone had put a glass in my hand and lifted it to my mouth. Unthinking, I swallowed the spicy, burning liquid all the way down. I could not imagine why the others were smiling and praising the drink. Alcohol must do something to change taste buds of those who use it frequently.

Other arms grabbed at me, the maids led by Alice.

"Let's head to the cliff edge and watch the sky colors as the sun rises. Hurry, Kenal." Brawny Tabitha held me steady.

I looked above to see few stars remained in the waning dark. Strangely, the drink opened my senses, the colors of the women's flower crowns glowed like candles.

Meanwhile, the family guests loaded into cars and carriages to view the Solstice from the heights above Slyme Gurney.

We servants gathered on the clifftop, well back from the brink, to wait for the first wink of the sun on the eastern horizon.

We needna wait long. Jane was first to see the exact spot of change. Soon we were jumping up and down and hugging one another. Then a human scream to the beat of falling rocks cut our joy.

"It's Alice," yelled Tabitha. "She must have stepped back too far."

I peered down to see her spread halfway down the cliff, stopped by an outcrop. She did not lie there like Mugwatch, all crookedy.

"I'll go fetch help while you find blankets and bandage materials. I hope she is not harmed," I shouted."

I ran back to the bonfire where a few men continued to drink and sing, nasty songs this time, of maidens not fair and sweet.

"Gleeves, Alice fell down the cliff. Take the roadster to fetch Mr Ileac. I think she's alive. The rest of you, find a way to get her up."

I then rushed about the follies to inform Lord Leo, but he was nowhere around. When I knocked on the Hedgehog, just Lord Sexsmith and his valet appeared, each rather disheveled. Returning to the manor entrance, I found Gleeves arriving with Mr Ileac.

When the doctor and I reached the clifftop, we found Turgid had worked ropes to reach Alice safely. He and a daily helpers were creating a body sling out of a quilt to lift her up.

"She's able to talk. She says she is sore and thinks perhaps only a wrist is broken from her attempts to break the fall."

Though twere frightening to watch, her ascent succeeded to bring her up safely.

"Alice, you gave us such terror," said Jane. "Here you were laughing, then screaming as you fell. Mr Ileac should soon be able to check for any breaks and bruises."

"I am now more shocked than anything. We were having such joy singing and dancing, when I stepped back into oblivion."

Sloth brought out a small container and fed it to her lips. I could smell the whisky.

"Sloth, she doesn't partake. Simple water will do."

"That's enough, Kenal. I decide whether to take this bitter cure. I want its sleeping draught."

After checking her limbs, Mr Ileac announced she had only sprains, and no broken bones.

Four of us carried her in the quilt down to Mrs Quirk's parlour, which had a day bed.

"You men needs must put the bonfire out. Alice is fine in my hands, "she advised.

Approaching the ritual area, Snerd cried out, "Oh, no, not another."

Csaba's bed was full aflame, with no sign of life within.

The corn dolls and reed animals, I thought, dry as faggots. Windy sparks could have set them off. The thick odor of roasted flesh made several of us gag.

We saw it were helpless to save the artist, but must put the fire out. Gleeves and Turgid ran to the stables to gather buckets to form a brigade from the lake. No one wanted to be last in line, close to the bed, so I volunteered. While dousing the bed, I saw the charred figure slowly take form. I didna imagine his terror, caught in the inferno while all of us were off taking care of Alice.

Tongues would be chittering all over Slyme Gurney tomorrow, once Mr Ileac showed up for his breakfast at the inn. He were a flap mouth.

Aware Euphoria, off with the gentry, had missed the crises, I stayed awake to inform her when she returned from the other Solstice group. Twere several hours before she arrived because they enjoyed a fine breakfast on the hilltop before dispersing.

When she drifted in, I be sitting in the entrance hall, dirty and exhausted. She knew something had happened. I tried to be as gentle as possible, by omitting the worst details. I said only that Csaba had died on the bed from loss of breath. That smoke smothered him, that his body was not recognizable, I left out. Nonetheless, Euphoria fainted. I rang for Jane to come up and revive her. Moved to the main saloon, Euphoria welcomed her tea, the eternal British medicine.

"Why did we do this," she cried. "It was fun in the beginning, but I could see people change with the dark. I worried it would not become a Shakespearean delight. Even the foxes were unusually noisy. Do you recall?"

"I do, ma'am. There were tricks of a bad kind. Someone slipped brandy into my punch. I heard there were chases and nasty games in the woods. Good Will Shake's charm in his midsummer play was simple by comparison, a man turned into a donkey. We forgot how even the best people have a sinful nature."

"Poor Letty! She was so fond of Csaba's instruction. Perhaps I should go to Cromwoh to share the news."

"His poor brother in Hungary, alone to face yet another family tragedy."

"Perhaps we can bury him here. Then I will always think of him and his love of Slanderley. I must ask Leo."

"What a sweet thought, milady. I wonder what his religious beliefs were. We shall know soon enough. I'm sure Jemima has already sent a cable."

On that note, I bowed and left the mourner to her privacy.

When I went to the main floor, I found now Sergeant Pepper with Constable Thyme. Given the odd circumstance of the death, they had already examined the bier and were questioning staff.

When it was my turn, I explained we had deserted Csaba to trace Alice's cries far off by the cliff. When we returned to find the bed aflame, we were helpless to save him and could only beat out the flames. We guessed that the bonfire, though some meters away, could have spit a spark into the dry straw. Had Csaba called out, none would have heard him.

Assured the guests had already left, and the servants altogether on the cliff path, the police eventually reported their agreement that no misadventure was involved. The medical examiner ascertained Csaba was unable to escape due to his injuries and an excess of alcohol. He also believed the man died from smoke inhalation very quickly and did not suffer during the burning. How he managed such conclusion given the frail bits of body is not my concern. His report did offer some relief to a crew guilty of leaving him alone in the field.

As it happened, Csaba's brother Ferenc responded that he would leave Tokaj immediately to come to Slanderley. He advised that the family was Catholic, yet he would welcome burial under a C of E service, for they would be similar were it not for the head-chopping king of old.

Two days later Ferenc leapt out of a cab by the front steps and ran up the stairs to ring the bell. I was down by the Summer House and happened to watch from afar. He was dressed in a kind of Hungarian green felt suit, a jaunty feathered hat. He seemed a taller version of Csaba, a bit dashing. Bunston welcomed him in, as was his due.

Entering to serve dinner later, I found Ferenc seated beside Lord Leo, who was extolling his admiration for Csaba, and his sorrow at the terrible loss. Obviously milord was playing a role, for we know he was not so fond of the wine salesman. Perhaps this common deception is what led Letty to speak of the household being full of lies. Children see the world in black and white, not the grey area where tact requires less than truth.

"He was such a kind teacher," chimed Euphoria. "We cannot imagine he will not show up again to give a lesson in the old nursery. Are you his only brother? Was there a sister?"

"Did he not tell you we were orphaned? No sister, alas. His paintings hang in our winery store. I will be sending messages to his many clients here and on the Continent. I know you were special to him as well, Miss Euphoria. He was grateful for your interest in the latest art that so many laugh at today. And for your hospitality, of course."

She dabbed her eyes while replying. "He was, I think, also a lonely man, being on the road so often. He knew he must do so for you and the winery, but it was not always a pleasant life. He was also a gentleman in every regard."

"Harumph. Yes, my dear departed wife, Lady Gladys, was of similar opinion," added his lordship through clenched teeth.

I wanted to interject how Csaba beguiled the women staff as well, but chewed on my lip instead. Oh, the weeping and wailing downstairs since his ill demise!

Jemima oversaw the funeral and burial plans. Csaba belonged to the Reformed Hungarian Church, so she found a local Chapel preacher to conduct the service in Slyme Gurney. Lord Leo offered a place in the family crypt, far from the de Loverly ancestors and adjoining the favorite hunting dogs. Ferenc poured a bottle of Furmint over the tomb, its rich honey aroma blessing the dankness.

The Slanderley Curse

Scatterings

A week after the funeral, I found Alice pulling suitcases from the storage room.

"I cannot stay here any longer. Three deaths in so few years. I am beginning to believe the Curse is real. I think you, Kenal, should put your ear out for a position elsewhere. You have fine skills now, and could leave this isolated, haunted place for a better position."

Her decision stunned me. "So are ye getting married soon? I thought you needed another year to have the money to start a household."

"Actually, I am going into service at Lord Rashcum's estate. The house keeper will be leaving within a year, and I will train to move into her position. It would be a wonderful advancement."

"What of your fiancé? Lord Rashcum's manor is far from your fiancé in Mothcannon."

"Csaba's murder had me thinking of what I want to do with my life. I prayed hard and asked for our Lord's guidance. The answer came clear, that I am not made for wedlock. I am too strong headed to submit to a husband."

"Have you told Mr Tiddlysquat? You've been together a long time."

"Nay, I'll tell him Sunday afternoon. I was beginning to think he wanted me more to oversee his business than commit to me out of strong feelings. He'd do better with a business partner or hiring someone who can be around hot coals all day."

"When do you leave then? We must have a farewell event to see you off."

"A week from Sunday. Mrs Quirk has already arranged for a gathering the night before. But you have not spoken to my suggestion, to leave here as well."

"Despite all that has happened, I find comfort here at Slanderley. Where else would I have the freedom of the library and my work with Mr Norton? The formal events are few, and the service runs smoothly. Also, I feel tied to Lord Leo, who saved me from the dreaded Grubbs."

"Work is no place to be so indebted. Did you go, Lord Leo would soon find a replacement and forget you."

"That is not all. I have saved my pence and shillings for future purposes. Csaba gave me the idea. I need not stay in Cornwall, or even England. My family has forgotten me, even me Mam, so I am free. My plan is to go when I am nineteen. Until then, I will pray for guidance, as you have."

"At that age you could have a boat and follow your family's trade. I'm sure your brothers would welcome you."

"There's too much risk and too little reward these days to be out with nets and hooks. We are entering a new era, and I want to join it."

"I wish you well. I trust you will send me a card now and then. I shall not forget you. Nae, I'll worry about you."

"We must trust the Lord, Alice. I am through with Lamentations. I canna forgive my enemies." She of course did not know of how Squimm and others troubled me. "And of course I shall send you notice of my adventures."

Ever willing to break custom, Lord Leo invited all to dine and say farewell to Alice in the large dining hall. He advised Mrs Viscous to create a buffet so no one be responsible to serve. He even shot some game birds for the feast, and sent Gleeves to Bude to purchase desserts from the fine bakery there. The preparation was the first real break in his grief over the loss of Lady Gladys.

I directed preparation of the tables, cutlery, and center pieces, while Bunston picked lesser wines from the cellar. We used the family's second service, so as not to spoil any of their best. Tabitha brought in yellowed linens from storage, apologizing for their dull appearance. Diggory ferreted a storage room for tarnished candelabra and centerpieces. Under fire light, the array would have passed the Bishop's wife's muster. We all felt most honored guests for the first time in our lives, so beloved was Alice.

We men could not help but serve the maids and such, for it were ingrained in us. Tabitha was a scullery maid, but tonight she were a duchess. We escorted them to the table and served them before treating ourselves. Lord Leo sat at the head of the banquet, with Bunston sitting beside. His lordship's face glowed lobster shell in the silvered candle light. When all had finished dessert, he stood to make a toast. While most had the wine, those among us more serious Chapel goers enjoyed a lemon water.

"We are here to bid adieu to Alice, whose talents are earning her future success in her new position. Were it possible, we would of course have offered a similar advancement. Both Mrs Quirk and I provided sterling recommendations for her. We shall miss Alice's many contributions to the calm functioning of the manor."

"Here, here." shouted Snerd while clinking his glass. "Let our master continue."

"Before you sit down, please refill, for I have another toast. I also thank all of you here, who have solaced me through (his voice breaking) the tragic loss of Lady Gladys." He brushed his right eye to emphasize his sorrow.

The honored guest blushed beetroot red. "Thank you, sir. It is I who must thank you for my happy years here. And this lovely party—I fear I am becoming speechless."

She looked around the room, taking in each of us one by one in her eyes as though to seal a photograph.

While Alice held us still, I noticed she had changed. Somehow I had missed her aging. Her light hair had darkened, her slim figure now softly padded.

Lord Leo clinked a glass to turn our attention. "Now I must retire early, while you continue to enjoy the remainder of the evening. I see more wine and puddings remain. Do finish them all. They do the cats no good."

With that farewell, he jerked out of his chair and fled the room. Lightening flashed his exit, with a rattling thunder close behind.

Still refusing spirits, I followed his orders and stuffed in a second pudding, a heavy cake with too many currants. Alice came over with her second dessert as well, a berry pie.

"So this is farewell, Kenal. I wish there were more time before I go. Mr Gleeves is taking me away before breakfast, for he is due to pick up some goods in Plymouth. I will miss our pleasant walks and talks of the Holy Book. May you find all you deserve, for you are an upright and honest man. I shall pray you one day find a wife of similar qualities."

"If she is half as good as you, Alice, I will be more than satisfied. Not that I am ready for marriage. I do want to see some of the world first. So many changes, so much speeding up."

"Aye, I understand. What worries me most is hints of conflict spoken about. Were there to be a war, you would be of age to fight. I hope I am wrong, for I cannot see you going off with a rifle. Or do you see it as your duty?"

"I trust the King will avoid such tragedy, just as he has improved our country's dealings with once enemies. Did he call me to battle, I would hope twere for a good reason. I lean toward peace through wise talk."

"I as well. I am sorry I must leave you now, for I've others to see before the evening ends." With that, she shook my hand, made a wan smile, turned, and went over to Mrs Viscous.

The servants' dining room were less cheery once Alice left. She had been the kind and fun older sister to me, as well as to others. Her modest manner kept the worst behaviors of Snerd and Turgid in check. Mr Bunston was near asleep, so did nothing to control the misbehaving men.

Imbibing leads to loud voices and rowdy singing. The noise tired me. Without any comment I slipped out the door and returned to my room.

There I grew very drowsy. Had Mrs Viscous added brandy to the pudding? I felt strangely drugged, and soon slid into a dreamless sleep, interrupted several times by a percussive storm rattling the windows.

Bright sun on my eyes startled me from my uneven slumber. Slipping on my night cloak, I went into the hall and up the back stairs to breathe in the air freshened by the rains. The storm clouds had moved on to the east. Drops sparkling on the shrubs and trees emitted tiny rainbow colors.

My life seemed ready for a new direction, one promising fulfillment and adventure. Alice was right, that I should think of my own future possibilities and not cling so to guilt or fear like a child.

Worse for the women, Jemima could not find a replacement, which added to their work. Jane was promoted to head maid, yet she were dim of mind and blank of eye. She were a hard worker, but neglected details, so the scullery maid was sent to follow behind and finish the leftover scrub or dust. Raised on cleanliness, I went up at times as well to add some polish or bring down a forgotten tray.

The family fell into gloom as well. Its members donned mourning colors even though Csaba had not been a family member. Euphoria tried to cheer Letty by continuing their painting together, but her landscapes were full of storm and haunt.

Twere a cable that took me briefly away from this bleak atmosphere.

MAM GONE. VERY SUDDEN. COME IMMEDIATELY.

Twas like a needle in the heart. Me Mam dead, and I not very close to her since my last visit. I had been resentful of her happiness in Mousehole, her doting on her grandchildren, my nieces and nephews. At the same time I mourned the Mam who loved me so, who wanted the best for me by sending me off to service. I knew it suffered her to lose her babe's companionship.

.There was no question I must leave. Much to my surprise, his lordship drove me in the car to the station where I could take the train south. I'd never ridden in a train before, and was sickened at first by the swirl of buildings and trees rushing by. Then the steady rock of the rails calmed me down, and I napped a bit. At Penzance, I found a carriage for sister's house.

The windows were darkened by drapery, a black ribbon hanging on the door. Before entering, I could hear the wails of a woman. Entering, I saw the cries were of a neighbor standing above the open coffin in the main sitting room. A niece ran up to me, "Uncle Kenal! See our gran is dead! She is dressed for Heaven!"

I hesitated to go and look, but a deep breath propelled me forward. Mam lied in her best dress, the blue of her closed eyes. Her face set a slight smile, while her hands crossed over her chest. Her wrinkled face were so smooth she seemed a young woman. I bent down to kiss her icy lips.

Soon I were surrounded by others of the family, who pulled me into the kitchen for a sup. Conan spoke up.

"The women were all here cleaning up, we men in the parlor. Mam said she needed to sit down a bit, so she took that chair by the hearth. They were so busy that they forgot about her. Done washing, they turned around and saw she was gone. She'd not said a word, just slipped away."

"Then I went to the carpenter to set to the casket. Of course he was prepared with pieces already cut. I chose the best in the selection and asked for four rope handles instead of two so we could carry her securely," added Goron. Meanwhile, the women laid her on the sofa to wash her and dress her in her burial clothes."

"I have something to place with her," I said, "the travel Bible she gave me, the one I read to her from. It has served me well, but I can leave it with her and get a new one."

"What a lovely thought, Kenal. You were her favorite."

"Tis true, though she were a good Mam to all. Look at us here, with no anger or jealousy between us. That be proof of her devotion."

People tramped in and out that day and the next, burials, deaths being so public and shared in our village. That is why my nieces and nephews did not hide away, but spoke frankly to visitors. One might join in with a wailer, then suddenly run off to play with a ball. The house was like that all the time, weeping and laughing and remembering.

On burial day, I grasped one of the rope holds with my brothers and my uncle, mam's only brother. As we wandered the streets to the graveyard, a parade grew behind us. I don't remember much about the service, apart from the hymns that broke out unplanned after the preacher spoke. "Deathless Spirit, Now Arise" and "When I Shall Reach the More Excellent Glory." I tried to join along, but thought more of her cold body, not her Angelic wings.

On leaving, I noted Mam's neighboring grave was Mr Creakle.

I stayed one more day at my sister's house, and could have stayed longer, but the house without Mam left me feeling less welcome. I was wrong, but didn't realize that until later. I was too caught up in my loss, ignored how my sisters and brothers felt the same.

On the train back, I thought of the silver pin Mam gave me, of Squimm and his theft. Blood rose to my face while I imagined finding him for revenge. I wanted the pin back to place in the grave, to trouble him according to the guidance from Lamentations. I recalled how Mam viewed the passage differently, and bit my hand to soften my hatred.

I had to take a coach westward from the train. It were so late at night that I quit when it stopped at Jamaica Inn. Because the night was moonless, I tripped and fell on the cobbles in the courtyard.

"Here, lad, take my hand." Another coach passenger, a short, wiry-haired man helped me up. "It's good the lights are on in the entrance way, which means we should be able to find a room for the night."

I followed him inside, surprised to see the rooms could have been from the ages ago. Heavy beams and dark cabinets gave the rooms a closed-in feeling, which left me feeling snug and warm. After signing in for a room, I went to warm up by the large hearth. Other men sat there, some drinking ale. The place little hinted of its history of smuggling and nasty types. Let's face it, smuggling was a longstanding part of our history, so the reference to the Inn protecting criminals is in the mind of outsiders, not we Cornwalligans.

My savior appeared as well and introduced himself as Phineas Phlurgh. He was on his way to Bude, but like me, decided to take a rest even though the distance was not so far.

"I have business there, you see. So I'm as well here as staying at a drafty room by the sea. And where do you be heading?"

"Not far away either. I am head footman at Slanderley, up the coast from Bude."

"Ah, yes, the cursed manor. I've heard you had another murder," spoke a portly old man. "Why do you work there? You're a fine specimen of a man and could find better labor anywhere in the country."

Phineas seconded. "It is a new world. I expect you started service young, when it seemed all that a poor lad could try."

"That is so," I answered, "but I have enjoyed my lot. The family is kindly and not harsh, as I understand many can be. I have even been able to work in the library and advanced my education on my own."

"See what I mean?" Phineas slapped his knee. "You must read the newspapers. You must know how opportunities are cropping up like weeds. I would hire you in a flash, could I have the position to do so."

"And what do you do, sir, doing business in Cornwall?"

"I deal in automotive goods. True, I travel now about the west of England, but I earn well and am saving to have my own automobile sales firm, which would also include farm machinery for the countryside. Cars are the future. Find a bit of the future and grab onto it now, early in the game!"

"Another salesman whom I met at Slanderley gave me almost identical advice. The truth is I have been thinking of leaving service and head to the Continent, where I have some connections. I have saved as well. I hope travel may help me find my clearest path."

"Wise lad," agreed the portly man. "I regret coming of age when the choices were fewer. At least my family was one of comfort, so I could go into law. Retired now."

As their conversation continued, I listened to these older men chat about trout fishing rivers, football teams, and which car was the best for rallies. They seemed optimistic, certain their lives would continue with diverse pleasures and success.

I realized the world was less split into the very rich and the very poor, that a man willing to look ahead and take chances could live a comfortable life, one of freedom. Lord Leo had endless comfort, yet he was also bound to traditions and his estate. Service bound me as well, yet with foresight I could shape a different life. Look at me brothers, who saw the collapse of fishing as an opportunity to make a better way for themselves.

My call was clear. I must commit to a different future and plan upon leaving Slanderley.

When I arrived at the manor the next day, I noticed a trunk in the hallway. Turgid was buckling the straps to hold it tight.

"What's that for?"

"His lordship and the others are leaving. They are moving to the London house."

"That's a surprise. When did this come up?"

"Lady Euphoria said it were time to take Letty away from this cursed place. Lord Leo agreed, and added he would join them. Algernon would do his school breaks there as well."

"It does make sense. Since Alice left, the caretaking has been less careful. I've heard others speak of leaving the manor as well."

"I myself am among them," replied Turgid. "There's an auto factory starting near my hometown, and I plan to work there once it opens. No more seven days a week! You could join me, Kenal. You are good with your hands."

"It is tempting, but I plan to travel across the Channel first before I decide upon my next position. I carefully saved me earnings, and was invited to visit Ferenc in Tokaj. Who knows, I may become a wine salesman."

After changing into work clothes, I joined Turgid in collecting and preparing the trunks and parcels for the family's journey. Most was being sent ahead, to be unpacked and ready upon their arrival in London a week later.

Several days later, Mr Bunston and Mrs Quirk announced changes in service caused by the departure of the family. Save themselves and Mrs Viscous, all house staff were advised to seek other situations. I could stay on as a general aide to the trio, from kneading bread to emptying bedpans. Naturally, I took the opportunity to announce my leave.

Here I were, packing and planning to leave, sooner than expected. What I would miss most was books. Though I knew I could swipe a few from the library, I couldna thieve. Books were everywhere in the world, and I would manage somehow.

I chose to leave the day of the family parting. We servants lined up in the main hall to give our farewells. It were a strangely quiet ceremony, with the merest nods and curtsies. Even Letty, now becoming a woman, kept a sober face. I realized she would be wed within five years or so.

To my surprise, Euphoria walked up to me to grasp my hand, dropping something within. It were me Mam's silver pin. She must have gotten it somehow from Squimm.

"Mam?"

"I have my ways, Kenal. Now go with God."

She turned to join the others. Little did I imagine I would never see her.

The Slanderley Curse

Abroad

You may think it strange I were ready to go abroad, me the fisherman's son. You likely forgot I became a man, one larger than my Tas or brothers, and secure in my body. I had gained many skills in service, along with further knowledge from work in the manor library.

Twere not an impulse. After Csaba died, I packed his belongings and gave them to his brother. Ferenc returned to me Csaba's travel sack, walking boots, and some clothes as thanks. They were of fine materials, such as I could never afford. He also returned Csaba's travel journal with its notes of places to stay and eat. Although it be written in Hungarian, I easily deciphered many of the entries, for a French or English hotel would be entered in its original language. Even better, Ferenc included Csaba's worn maps, which were also marked up with his pathways.

I wrote to Ferenc of my sometime arrival. I didna expect to be able to journey so soon, nor I expect, did he. I faced a long journey before I could reach the vineyards on the Tizsa.

Following a final hearty meal with Mrs Viscous and the remaining staff, I swung up my pack and left for Mousehole. I decided to surprise my family to tell them of my plans in person.

They welcomed me as an invited guest, someone to break the daily pattern. My nephews and nieces were full of wise questions and less full of play. I could see they were well-schooled and saw a world beyond the small port. For several weeks I enjoyed their companionship and that of my sisters and brother, our lively talk at meals followed by singing and long walks.

When I explained my plans to cross the Channel, they were not surprised. They understood how my life at Slanderley exposed me to people with broader experience. They were also relieved I was leaving that house of death. The day I departed, Goron handed me a heavy purse to ease my travel. I promised to return, that I hoped to settle in Mousehole with a family one day. He did not believe me, but I were true.

Of course I trod the hill to the small cemetery to honor me Mam (and Mr Creakle.) I told her I was wearing the pin, that a good person found it and returned it to me. It were to be my protector as I went into foreign lands. I spoke aloud for a while, apologized for being less than honest in my letters home. When I begged her forgiveness, a shaft of light flared on her stone. I know, you think me caught up in Cornish fantasy, but it is true, the light, a sign from above the earth.

I departed from Penzance on a trading boat to land in Brittany. I were supposed to help crew, but what humiliation. I discovered I lacked sea legs, and was soon hanging over the wale with green pallor. So much for my childhood desire to be a fisherman. Did my parents know early on that I was tied firm to land? Whatever, I had to pay after all for the crossing and was first off the boat.

From there I headed eastward, often riding in farm carts, and staying in villages or farm sheds. I were comfortable in the countryside, where the people were blunt and hardworking. Did I see someone at work, I'd come on and help out. That kindness often led to a warm meal and loft bed. Taking my time, I went from hand signals to minimal Froglish. Despite the farmers' welcome, I did not want to linger and delay my journey.

Eventually I ended up near Dijon. Twere almost August, when the French flee the cities for their country chateaus and old farm hovels. By then I stank from the road and decided to enjoy a few days in a proper city hotel. I passed from hilly vineyards down to the town center with its inviting old buildings, signs of the village from which it grew. There I settled in a quiet lodging to bathe and rest. I also continued this account begun several years ago.

Ferenc responded to my cable with a cheerful note. He noted the grape harvest would start soon, and he needed every hand available. I were welcome to join in and learn more about the process. He knew I would not quaff from the cellars, thus be inclined to accident.

His invitation sent me packing and plotting of the fastest way to Tokaj, a good distance yet to travel. When I learned of a train that tracked the Rhine, I continued through Basel and disembarked at Konstanz to sleep in a bed. The next morning, I felt a chill, the start of a summer cold, and decided to remain in this warm little city before heading across Austria. The lodge keeper's wife brought up broths and herbal teas to speed my recovery. I wanted to move on, but knew I'd be no help to Ferenc were my health not fully returned.

So it were a surprise to hear a knock on the door in the middle of the night.

"Herr Gundry. Wachet auf! Wir uns im Krieg befinden."

"War? With English?"

"Ja. Gehen Sie in die Schweiz. Nun."

"Now? How?"

She pulled out the local tourist map and pointed to the way to the bridge over the lake. If I continued through the old town, I would soon be in Switzerland.

I had no choice. War! I was an enemy and could not chance what might happen if I remained in Germany. I thanked her with extra payment, bundled up, and went out into the misty night. Others crowded the street, like me, with rucksacks or suitcases, and heading toward the border. I heard various languages, for no one could be sure what the start of conflict would mean for one's country. We rushed as a crowd into adjoining Kreuzingen, then scattered throughout that now safe little city.

I huddled in a doorway to nap until the sun came up. The aroma of coffee led me to a café open for the early workers. I sat down at a tiny table in a corner with my tea and pastries. My brain shot frightening scenarios at me. Should I travel on to Hungary or return home? What about money? Just what was this war about? Would I get caught in the destruction?

During my leisurely passage thus far, I had not read newspapers, given I didn't know the languages well. Similarly, I could not understand conversations about recent events. Foolish was I.

Then I noticed a well-dressed, silver-haired man several tables over holding an English paper. He was smoking and frowning over the print. Perhaps he could help me.

When I approached, he put the paper down and gave an inquiring look.

"Excuse me, do you speak English? I just fled Konstanz and know nothing of the war."

His response was quick. "Of course. my fellow. Do sit and join me." He pushed out a chair and called the waiter over to refill our drinks. "Frederick Pharynx."

"Kenal Gundry. I apologize for my appearance. I have been on the road for weeks and was hesitant to interrupt you."

"Not at all. I have been travelling as well. This paper is two days old, sent by my employer. Thus have I been informed all along since I left England late July. Now, what do you want to know?"

"Who is fighting? I gather we just got involved against Germany, which is why I had to flee Konstanz in the middle of the night."

His reply was clear and well-organized, though the actual circumstances confused me, as they involved the late June murder of the heir to the Austro-Hungarian throne, an assassin from a country I had never heard of. Within a month Germany struck out in support and set upon Russia, Belgium, France, and Luxemburg. Their neighbor allies besieged, England joined the fray. Even with his pointing to spots on a map, I was confused by the vast size of the conflict.

"How can our little island country be of much help?"

He smiled while lighting a cigarette. "We will show the Germans what fools they are to start this war. The government will have all the young men signing up and soon in battle. The generals assured the PM the fighting will be over quickly. Once we cross the channel, our allies will stiffen their bravery and we shall plow over the enemy."

"Are you a journalist? You seem to have inside information."

"No, though I do have knowledgeable friends. Now, shall you not want more to eat? I can take you to my lodgings afterward, where you will find a bed and security. You need time to think about your future. I have a son your age who is likely preparing to enlist as we speak. He has already cancelled his next Oxford term, to my delight."

Whoever Pharynx was, I decided to trust him and accepted his invitation. He led me to a three-bedroom flat on the first floor of an ancient building looming above a back street.

"The company owns this for its travelers. I'm the only one staying here for now, though I will likely be called back home soon. Meanwhile, do enjoy the facilities. The kitchen is well-stocked, and we enjoy a daily maid. Now I am off. See you for a late meal, perhaps."

While attempting to sleep, I became wary. Why was this man so hospitable to a Cornwall man? He was clearly very nationalistic, proud his son was planning to fight. Did he intend to take me back to do the same? I must be very careful.

When I awoke from a deep sleep, the rooms were dark and he was not in. After turning on lights, I went about looking for information—opened drawers and closets, but found only basic items. His bedroom was locked, and I was not going to force anything.

I found enough food in the ice box to make a dinner of ham and potatoes, which I warmed in the oven, and followed that with a slice of a rich chocolate cake. I waited for Mr Pharynx's return, but he did not appear.

Once full, I calmed down. He was posh and secretive, perhaps also lonely, being away from England. Recent events were making me confused and indecisive. At least I could spend a few days here while I planned my next move. With Hungary cut off, I must either return home or find a way to survive in the neutral safety of Switzerland.

Apart from a few guidebooks on the country and some maps, the bookshelves were bare. The next day I used these to learn more about the country and find a possible a solution to my problem. My key lack was not skill, but language. I decided to settle in Geneva with its lake and distance from Germany. Meanwhile I must be out among the locals and listen to their speech.

Mr Pharynx did not return the second or third nights, though the maid arrived promptly at ten each morning. She did not seem surprised to see me.

The fourth night, I woke midst a deep sleep to hear voices in the other rooms. To my shock, I also heard the lock on my door turned shut from the outside. I were trapped.

So my fears were not without a basis. Who was Mr Pharynx? Why did he imprison me?

Of course he could not succeed. I moved like a snake to gather my few goods, tied a sheet to the bed frame, opened a window, and lowered myself down the one story to the ground. I landed in a narrow side yard and crept to peek around the front corner to the street. There I saw two large black roadsters, one still with a chauffeur. Tiptoeing to the back of the building, I worked my way over a fence, into an alley, and ran as fast as possible from that demonic flat.

My memory being good, I recalled the general location of the train tracks, headed that way, and soon found myself at what the Swiss called the *bahnhof*. A train had just pulled in, heading toward Geneva. Just in time, I had a ticket and found an empty compartment. It were a local, slow train, yet I didn't mind, for I fell fast asleep, to awaken in my chosen city.

Arriving during the bustle of the morning, I soon felt at ease. The voices spoke in French, which I knew just enough to read the signs and ask for help. Second, the hilly streets overlooked a large swath of water, Lac Leman, and the air wafted a breeze strangely oceanlike. I felt safe, being so far from the nasty Germans. Though living on the edge of France, the residents behaved without sign of concern a war was brewing.

I wandered into the old city with its narrow lanes and medieval buildings. Such places stirred my imagination. I recalled from school that the city was known as the Protestant Rome, thanks to Calvin, and searched for the Cathedral where he preached. It was like a

Greek temple on the outside, but resembled our English stone wonders inside. It were chilly, so I just glanced about and left to find some tea and hearty meal. My stomach full, I located a lodging and spent the late afternoon napping.

There were worst places to spend a war.

I'd a full purse and more, thanks to lifting some funds from Mr Pharynx. You don't think I snooped just for information, did ye? Before you point your finger, reflect on my fate, isolated by history, away from friends and family. War makes desperate acts.

After some weeks of flitting about the town and surrounding hills, I grew bored. I needed something to steady my ways or I could be tempted to enter the sinful part of town and fall into degradation.

Though I could readily locate a position at a grand house, I did not want to return to service. As happens to the traveler, a chance encounter solved my need. I was wandering a back alley and came upon a motor car repair place. Poking around the small parking area, I heard someone speak from behind.

What follows is a more refined version of our conversation, which was a mix of halting attempts in one another's language, assisted by gestures and grunts.

"Bonjour. Do you like that one? It will be for sale soon. The owner, like many of our young men, is off to France."

Turning around, I faced a mechanic in his work suit, a spanner in his hand. He was shorter than me, with crinkly dark eyes and a small groomed mustache.

"Bonjour. I can only wish. It is a fine roadster, though it tends to lean too much on curves."

"You know your autos. You seem young to be so aware. I'm Toulouse Jaune.

"Merci. Kenal Gundry, from Cornwall. I spent my youth in service at an estate where the master and his friends took up autos. They were like children with toys. I became interested as well, and often spent time with the mechanic and eventually assisted him. I saw the future was in autos. It is a dream of mine to have my own roadster."

"What happened? Why are you here and not fighting for England?"

"The family left the estate and I decided to explore an invitation to learn about wine in Hungary. I was on my way when the war broke out, and private concerns forced me to stay in Switzerland. I am not a coward, if you are thinking that."

"Ah, no. I have no thought on this war except it is filling fields with the blood of young men. Come and see what I am working on now."

He led me into a space fit for only two cars. The tools were all arranged neatly on the walls and cabinet tops. Even the floors were clean, with sawdust over an oil spot to absorb the stain.

The car was a four-cylinder Delage. It looked brand new, though I knew it was several years old.

"What a beauty," I said. "Someone has taken good care."

"The owner, Madame Pimplemouse, does not go out much. She has her chauffeur bring it in on schedule, whether it needs it or not. I am just tightening a few joints."

"Her chauffeur seems a lucky man. He must do other work for her as well."

"No at all. And worse, he has a large flat above the remodeled carriage house that once kept several horse stalls. I think he is a distant nephew, a bounder. One learns much about people in my business. So what is your business on this fine afternoon?"

I told him how I had chosen to take time to learn the city and improve my French, that I expected to find work soon, perhaps at a restaurant or hotel. I watched him work, admired the ease of his manner. He explained how his father owned the first machine shop to meet the needs of growing small industry. He was married with two children of school age.

I was about to leave, when he offered his hand. "Could you think about working for me? My last assistant and I parted ways last month. I cannot provide full-time, but I see from your clothes that you are frugal. You can always find some serving work when you want such."

His offer left me stunned, unable to respond.

"I apologize. I am presumptuous to think a healthy lad would accept my position when the city is so in need of your sort and offering much more payment."

"No, it is not that. It is just that I had not considered a break from waiting on others. I gladly accept your offer."

Thus I spent the war, toughening and bruising my hands as I assisted Toulouse in his shop. I moved to a better lodging, found a church that preached to my liking, and acquired fluent French. I made a few male friends with whom I hiked in the challenging countryside. Sometimes I enjoyed a walk or luncheon with this or that pert young woman, but I was not drawn to any particular one. None matched Alice.

In time, I had a new love, the beat-up car I bought and rebuilt on my free days. It was nothing special, but it promised me freedom to drive to Hungary when the war ended.

I knew Hungary was not a key battle area, yet I worried about Ferenc. Though he was too old to be conscripted, I expected he was not as comfortable as I was in my Swiss cocoon. The grapes needed tending, war or not. Then in late 1917 I received an envelope with broad black edges, commonly used for death announcements.

Translated by a friend, it read:

Dear Gundry Kenal,

I regret to inform you my beloved Ferenc died last week. He was working deep in the wine cave making repairs when a   group of loose rocks fell on him, killing him instantly. He has already been buried in the local church cemetery.

Given this terrible shock, I am leasing the winery to a neighbor and moving to Debrecen, where my daughter lives.

Please know that Ferenc was looking forward to your arrival and participation in the vineyard. I pray you find a

*similar situation for your talents now that this opportunity
is gone.*

In sorrow,

His fiancée, Jolie

I sent off my condolences and some memories of Ferenc at Slanderley. Too sad, both brothers dead in the prime of their lives. Well, the Lord giveth and he taketh away.

Not many months later, the war ended. Despite Geneva's charm and my satisfying job, I longed to return to Cornwall, its seas, and its ancient ruins. I longed for Cornish food and Cornish voices.

I imagined starting my own repair shop in a large town. I had learned how to run the business and saved enough for the tools and fixings. I made an uneventful trip by driving through southern France, eventually ferrying over the Channel, and crossing Britain into Plymouth. There I made lease on a perfect location for my project and arranged for some storage to be built.

Meanwhile, I must do my Prodigal Son duty. I owed Lord Leo apology and appreciation for all he had done for me. I wanted more news of my fellow workers and of Letitia and Euphoria. Perhaps I could even see Alice as well. Hoping Slanderley were once again occupied, I headed there.

Twere a surprisingly sunny day when I drove into Slyme Gurney. People crowded around when I parked by the pub.

"Kenal, we thought you were dead. "

"Gundry, look at ye. So large and healthy. What happened to the scrawny servant?"

"Betsy, come see. He's back. Won't the girls be fighting over him?"

"How'd you get that auto? You've come up in the world, my lad."

It couldn't have been a better welcome. They followed me into the pub, where I ordered a pint for all. I were still true to my refusing pledge and had berry water.

In little time I learned the manor house was being prepared for the de Loverly family's return from London in another week. Turgid and Digorry each died in the trenches, while Snerd and Sloth hid in the isolation of the estate. Bunston ended up serving a General in London and never saw action. Word of Alice was that she never married and ran a congenial hold over her maids. I thought to surprise her at her church on some Sunday.

Even without the Devil's brew, I were abeam with happiness.

I were laughing with Jimson, the pub owner, when a firm hand grasped my shoulder and turned me around. Constable Mustard.

"So you've come back to pay your dues, Gundry? I have a nice little cell for you. I'm charging you with the murder of Csaba Szarka. Make way everyone, please, and say farewell. You'll not see this one again."

"Ye must be wrong," shouted Jimson, who came out from behind the bar and put his hands on my shoulders. He and Mustard struggled for control of me until another man pulled Jimson off.

"We know Kenal is a good man. Let the courts settle this out. He will soon be free."

A familiar voice popped in, Sloth. "A joke on us, Kenal. We couldn't resist."

When my heart calmed down, he assured me Lord Leo was at the manor. I took a room at the Inn and wrote my old employer in hope of an appointment.

The response was most pleasant. Lord Leo invited me to dine with him privately at an inn table in an alcove where none could hear us. We spoke of the war, its terrible destruction. I recounted my adventure and life in Geneva. Over dessert, his lordship leant in close.

"I must be honest with you. I am open to the possibility you did set Csaba's bed aflame. The men's jest on you was based on gossip."

"Do you see any truth in that? I could have nothing to do with that ghastly demise."

He looked down at the table and took his time to answer. "I do not doubt your innocence. Let us face facts, though. Your role in Lady Gladys's death. I know you planted the glove that pointed to Thelma Grubb as murderer. That saved a lot of trouble."

"I'm not sure I understand."

"I'm sure you do."

He stood abruptly, crushed his cigar, and left. I never saw him again.

I'd write more, except my energy is waning. My life dreams fade. I am abed in my Plymouth flat, a storm wailing, while I wait for my promised land. I came down with the wretched flu that is slicing off so many around the world. To guarantee my life among the angels, I make a quick confession here.

Lord Leo was right to mistrust me. I lured Mugwatch to the Ha-ha that foggy night and shoved him to his death. He arrived very late and very tired. I did not go to sleep, but hid in a side room until he entered ours. Then I rushed in to say we needed to check the lawn, that some large dog were out chasing the two rams still outside. Twere nonsense, of course, and easy to misdirect him on such a moonless, misty night. I were sure he'd done Alice's botherings. That he wasn't was a small error on my part.

As for Lady Gladys, the day after her death I found grit from the cliff path when I collected Lord Leo's boots. Determined to save him from Thelma Grubb, I planted the glove on the slope several days after the discovery of the body. She had left both gloves behind during her quick departure after the auto party. I found them tucked in a sofa cushion when I was straightening the main saloon. She had so flirted with Lord Leo that I had good reason to kill her to protect him. The gloves gave me another option. Murder by secondhand.

I were the cause of Csaba's demise. Recall someone pranked Alice and me by pouring brandy into our drinks during Midsummer. In my drunken state, I found a still-lit cigarette butt on the ground and tossed it at the bed. I were sure of his botherings of the maids. Not that they were totally innocent, those Whores of Babylon. Had war not interfered, the scullery maid would have collapsed from one of my special concoctions. I had my little list and much patience to space the deaths.

Is not murder one of the Sacred Ten? How be I so cruel, you ask. Oh, but our Savior is forgiving of those who confess, and so I leave this wicked world prepared for the choir of angels.

The Slanderley Curse

Epilogue

When the police entered to investigate the gruesome odor emanating from his cottage, this journal was found in Mr Gundry's lap. The Constable who removed it put it in an evidence locker and forgot it. His family, notified to collect his belongings, heard nothing about it. They buried him near his mother at the Mousehole Cemetery.

Gundry likely caught the Spanish Flu from Lord Leo de Loverly, who died at Slanderley. His mistress, Gertrude Quirk, also fell to the mortal flu and was buried nearby him.

The estate was under lawyers' control until Algernon came of age. His sister Letitia and Aunt Euphoria were fortunately spared infection.

Years later, a clerk at the Plymouth police station discovered the journal in evidence storage. Realizing it was of no use for any cases, he glanced through to notice frequent references to Slanderley. On that basis, he sent it to the estate, where Bunston delivered it to the estate archives.

By chance, Oxford student Horton Hoot was busy cataloguing new arrivals and contacted his advisor, Chippy Norton, now a don at Pembroke. Norton had already published a study of the curious development of the estate since its origins, *Cornish Law and the*

Decline of Slanderley. He was naturally excited to hear of the account and rushed down to study the manuscript

After reviewing the contents, Norton ordered the journal packed away and restricted from access. He prepared a brief description for the Archive Guide in case any future researcher wished to examine the manuscript, but none was allowed to do so while Norton lived.

Having lived at Slanderley during periods of time Kenal Gundry served, I can speak authentically to its value. Alas, it is the deceptive memoir of a poorly schooled, naïve youth from an overly pious fishing family.

As a result of his extreme Methodist leanings, Gundry viewed the world with its heretical Orthodoxy. His piety fed a tendency toward suspicion and paranoia. He also inflated his role among his superiors, such as Lady Euphoria and Lady Letitia. As for his account of Thelma Grubb, I can only point to his base anti-Americanism. I could spend pages pointing to related biases in his thought, but merely warn readers of his self-promoting intentions. Such is true of so many memoirs. In the ladder of service, he was but a shrew puttering about the background.

As noted within, I did try to befriend and advise him away from his extreme parochialisms. I admit he was bright and quick to learn, but his narrow upbringing and Chapel beliefs stunted his potential.

Perhaps most egregious is his preoccupation with the so-called "curse." True, many fell to strange fates at the estate, and have done recently as I write. His curiosity merely reflects the backwardness of Cornwall culture, its romance with pixies and dark forces. Rational people will understand the presence of sheer coincidence providing the basis for folk tales. Thus my own eminent volume on estate history ignores any mention of this nonsense.

Reader, beware.

Chippy Norton, Pembroke, Oxford

Graced with viewing the manuscript decades later, I must point to biases in Mr Norton's evaluation. Historians today no longer discount folk tales and myths as irrational. Too often a deep reading within the context of the era reveals elements of truth. Archaeologists have found early stories of floods passed orally in a culture without calendar dating are able through scientific study to document the presence of deluges in that distant past.

I reject the Curse as superstition or folly. If things are believed to be real, they are real in their consequences. Enough people in the Slyme Gurney area believed in the Curse, which made it convenient for potential malefactors. In a sense, Gundry himself perpetuated in the spread of the Curse, albeit using his religious beliefs to sanction his own ill behavior.

Indeed, I am not convinced Gundry acted as he claimed. That he killed Mugwatch, perhaps, him being a man of little piety thought to be bothering Alice.

Although his account of killing Csaba rings true, I deem it vainglory to seem a knight in armor protecting service women. If he were at the cliff edge to watch the sunrise, exactly when did he flick the cigarette ash? More likely, a spark from the fire accidentally set the bed afire.

As my forthcoming study will show, nuns, badly treated, similarly found themselves driven to unholy behaviors. Sister Labia did exist and did know Lord Albert, which is not to mean she had any role in his gruesome death. That Lady Gladys found solace in later nuns' piety and practices would have provoked her husband beyond her inclination to Roman Catholicism. He knew of the Curse, after all, and the key role of a nun in its reputed creation. So, who knows? Was she pushed by her husband or on her husband's orders? Being a mere scholar, I leave the solution to others.

Thelma Grubb, the suspected murderer of Lady Gladys, did escape the law. In 1925, she was located in Guadalajara, where she was married to a grandee of some sort, Senor Gusano, and again enjoyed the life of leisure. By then, British authorities believed too much time had passed and with key witnesses dead to seek her extradition and trial. Her husband died in 1926, after which she disappeared with all the wealth of his estate. So Gundry's revengeful attempt to see her hang never happened. .

As for his nemesis in Konstanz, Frederick Pharynx, I located him for an interview. He was vice president for a British company, and busy closing up European ties. The night Gundry fled, Pharynx was merely commandeering his team to hasten them safely to England. He locked the bedroom door temporarily so his colleagues would not awaken Gundry. Pharynx was surprised Gundry's false suspicions led him to escape the apartment.

The Curse continues to haunt Slanderley. I wish I could say life on the estate calmed down under Lord Algernon's rule, but as readers of scandal sheets know, this has not been the case. Lady Gladys was not the last wife to die under mysterious circumstances. The lawyers once again argue over who is to inherit the manor and its holdings. This being recent history, I absolve myself from further discussion.

Dame Cecelia Scrivener
Winterfield College, Oxford University

The Slanderley Curse

Acknowledgements

In thinking about a prequel to *Love and Death in Slanderley*, I further immersed myself in the history of Cornwall. One again, Daphne du Maurier served well, this time through her homage, *Vanishing Cornwall,* with photographs by her son Christian. A.K. Hamilton Jenkin's *Cornwall and Its People* proved fine social history with its accurate and unsentimental accounts of daily life. Based on three separate studies published in the early 1930s, he lived closer in time to the experiences of seafarers and miners. He was astute enough to include folk tales and strange beliefs without discussing them as oddities or proof of cultural inferiority.

With Covid preventing a return trip to Cornwall, I benefitted by a weeklong online course through Road Scholar. The usual hiking guides, Peter Maxted and Heather Newman, provided a visually rich overview, albeit of more popular spots for visitors. They especially elaborated the natural world, botany and geology, in addition to the arts. This led to reading Maxted's *The Natural Beauty of Cornwall.*

I often referred to two guidebooks. The Ordnance Survey's *Leisure Guide to Cornwall* not only offered a gazetteer and fine maps, but details of walks in particular parts of the county. Michelin's *The West Country of England* helped place the peninsula within the context of that segment of England overall, notably the key boundary with Devon.

I scanned British newspapers online for Cornish journalism during the Edwardian Era. They also familiarized me with locals' information about national activities, notably the activities of King Edward VII. One story led to the description of the catastrophic storm of the first chapter. The glasslike sherds falling from the sky were in the news account.

Local historical societies, particularly those that digitized information. For example, through one I viewed photographs of Mousehole taken at the time of the story. The internet also led to maps of towns from the period as well.

I thumbed the King James Bible often. The Lamentations quote was unplanned, selected at random when it was time for Kenal to read to his mother.

I did not read the adventures of Poldark, nor view the series on television.

The character of Kenal emerged full born. I often felt I was channeling him, that I could go to Mousehole and find his grave.

This book is a prequel to *Slanderley: Love and Death in Cornwall.* The de Loverly family members and the Quirk sisters are the center of the story following WWI. Algernon becomes Lord of the Manor, while Letitia matures and marries a local. In draft, the sequel *Slanderley at War* picks up the WWII experiences of Letitia.

Covid challenged the lives of many. In my case, its emergence coincided with a terminal diagnosis for my husband, Michael Ford

Orton. On our first road trip, forty years ago, I read aloud from a manuscript while he drove through deserts and mountains. He was my greatest fan, though truth be told, I doubt he read all my books. Our introduction to Cornwall was a car breaking down. Left to wait several days for the part to arrive, we relaxed in the quiet fishing village and inhaled the seafaring life of the inhabitants. We continued on, and especially enjoyed the moors with their rich physical evidence of deep history.

I knew another writing project would center me while Mike's disease progressed, the treatments causing more discomfort than the disease. His turn was sudden, and what we planned for, in the peace of the house and his family in the summer of 2021. He was happy to hear I was into another Slanderley book, and I regret he was unable to see its completion.

Susan Salenger was a constant support following my husband's death. We commiserate over recent widowhood and the adventures of publishing.

And to those who showed up when most needed: Barbara Lesch McCaffry and Mac McCaffry; Cski, AKA Carol Lewandowski; Jane Skoler, Bernie and Railey Album; Gary McKinnon, and Jeffrey Grove. Caroline McKinnon gave her professional understanding of grief.

Longtime friend Cristina Olsen was my key content and line editor. Her detailed and astute questions pushed me to develop certain characters and episodes more fully. Any inconsistencies and errors are my own.

Special thanks to ever-shedding feline Misty for companionship in my new solitude. As always, to my daughter M. Kendra Stoll, for her care and support.

Clarice Stasz

claricestasz.com

\

About the Author

Clarice Stasz grew up in South Jersey, raised by a naturalist father and art-loving, Phillies fanatic mother. She graduated from Douglass College when it was all-women. She earned graduate degrees from the University of Wisconsin and Rutgers University. There followed a post-doctorate award to study African American history at Brown University.

Stasz is Emerita Professor in History at Sonoma State University. She has won awards from the National Endowment for the Humanities, American Association for the Advancement of Science, Rockefeller Archives, and Sonoma State University.

She has written professional articles and books on simulation and gaming in the classroom, gender roles, racial inequality, and social control. Her general audience books explore the underplayed contributions of women from the Vanderbilt and Rockefeller families. Her other ongoing study explores the life and times of Jack London and his extended family. She is editor of London.sonoma.edu, a general resource on the writer and activist.

The Slanderley Curse

The Slanderley Curse

The Slanderley Curse